THE SPACE BETWEEN

LARRY HINKLE

ISBN: 978-1-68510-121-3 (sc)
ISBN: 978-1-68510-122-0 (ebook)

First printing edition: February 16, 2024
Printed by Trepidatio Publishing in the United States of America.
Cover Artwork: Don Noble
Edited by Sean Leonard
Proofreading, Cover Layout, & Interior Layout by Scarlett R. Algee

Trepidatio Publishing, an imprint of JournalStone Publishing
3205 Sassafras Trail
Carbondale, Illinois 62901

Trepidatio books may be ordered through booksellers or by contacting:
or
JournalStone | www.journalstone.com

Between will lure you in and have you unwittingly ratcheting up the intensity with every page. And that's when Hinkle sinks his literary claws in, leaving you captivated and wanting more." – Rena Mason, Bram Stoker Award®-winning author of *The Evolutionist* and *The Devil's Throat*

"A wonderfully sinister collection, packed with evil humor and twist endings galore! Hinkle describes himself as a 'painfully unknown' author, but this book will change that. Very highly recommended." – Jeff Strand, Bram Stoker Award®-winning author of *Twentieth Anniversary Screening*

"Larry Hinkle is a gem. And, yes, it's probably a cubic zirconia, but he brings a distinct voice to the horror comedy sub-genre that readers will absolutely love." – Bridgett Nelson, Splatterpunk Award-winning author of *A Bouquet of Viscera*

"This is because I dropped you on your head as a child, isn't it?" – Larry's Mom

Advance Praise for *The Space Between*

"Larry Hinkle's *The Space Between* is an everyman's collection of uncanny twisted little tales exploring the weird in corn fields, quarries, quarks, and other creepy corners of the world. With a voice that is irreverent, unexpected, and delightfully macabre, Hinkle is an author to watch. Go on. Step into the tunnel. What could possibly go wrong?" – Lee Murray, five-time Bram Stoker Award®-winning author of *Grotesque: Monster Stories*.

"Reading the stories of Larry Hinkle is like being in a room with all your favorite people: each one is different—colorful and abrasive in their way—and you love them all for that, and for the fantastic adventures they take you upon." – Eric J. Guignard, multiple award-winning author and editor of *That Which Grows Wild* and *Doorways to the Deadeye*

"From bogey men and garbage monsters to time loops and socially-awkward cannibals, *The Space Between* highlights Hinkle's gift for tongue-in-cheek whimsy and spine-tingling terror. Each story is a delight!" – Patrick Freivald, Bram Stoker Award®-nominated author of *In the Garden of Rusting Gods*

"*The Space Between* is a collection of cosmic and comedic tales that are as beautiful as they are unnerving. Hinkle is not simply an author: he's a consummate storyteller." – Rebecca Rowland, author of *White Trash & Recycled Nightmares*

"This collection is a mix of classic horror, cosmic horror, and grand weirdness. Nostalgic, entertaining, and unsettling—these stories were easy to fall into, harder to escape." – Richard Thomas, Bram Stoker, Shirley Jackson, and Thriller Award finalist

"Larry Hinkle's *The Space Between* offers up horror in a multitude of subgenres—all of which will leave you breathlessly turning the page to the next one. Some funny, some gory, some futuristic, and some weird AF, it's hard to pick a favorite, especially when Hinkle expertly sets these tales within his own universe. Do not miss out on this up-and-comer in the horror world!" – EV Knight, Bram Stoker Award®-winning author of *The Fourth Whore*

"Larry Hinkle's *The Space Between* is a an aptly named collection of short stories that range from dark and mysterious to absurd, from creepy to frightening, and from fantastical to gritty. I absolutely loved it! You can't go wrong with any of these joyfully demented pieces. *The Space Between* proves beyond a shadow of a doubt that Larry Hinkle is cementing his place in horror fiction and doing it like nobody else." – JG Faherty, author of *Ragman*, *The Wakening*, and *Sins of the Father*.

"Larry Hinkle's debut collection takes you to some really dark places with maniacal glee. Stabbing you while you smile then kicking you in the teeth, half this collection is so delightfully wicked it'll have you laughing yourself into an early grave. The other half is likewise fantastic, masterful horror that spawns the full range of human emotion and, of course, fear. Horror-comedy and just plain horror at its finest." – Jason Parent, author of *Eight Cylinder* and *The Apocalypse Strain*

"Gory, inventive, and blisteringly funny, Larry Hinkle's *The Space Between* is a sit-up-and-take-notice kind of debut. Killer clowns, sentient garbage dumps, and evil imaginary friends abound, as does horror, humor, and a whole lot of heart. *The Space Between* is definitely one you'll want to make space on your shelf for!" – Christa Carmen, Bram Stoker Award®-nominated author of *The Daughters of Block Island*

"A Larry Hinkle story will stab you in the heart and put a smile on your face at the same time. This long-awaited collection will introduce new readers to his delightfully diabolical style, and it is cause for celebration!" – Douglas Ford, author of the award-winning *Little Lugosi (A Love Story)*

"Hinkle takes his reader by the hand and deftly guides them from one darkly strange journey to the next in *The Space Between*, a collection that treats the reader to some wickedly gruesome delights and surprisingly bittersweet moments in time with plenty of twists and turns along the way. I loved every bit of this!" – Kenzie Jennings, author of *Reception* and *Always Listen to Her Hurt*

"A phantasmagoric odyssey through the void, with each new story a fresh feast of delicious madness." – Wile E. Young, Splatterpunk Award winning author of *The Magpie Coffin*

"Hinkle is a master at settling you in with the people and places of that all too familiar hometown. But be warned, ghastly horrors await! *The Space*

CONTENTS

PUBLICATION HISTORY

ACKNOWLEDGMENTS

Where to begin? How about with you, for taking a chance on a debut collection from a relatively unknown (okay, painfully unknown) writer? There are tons of books you could've spent your money on, and the fact that you chose mine over one by Tom Deady means a lot. Really.

I can't remember a time I didn't want to be a writer, but I certainly remember when I decided I didn't have what it took to be one. It was in a creative writing class at THE Ohio State University sometime during the mid-eighties. Everyone in class fancied themselves a "literary writer." Except me. I wrote pulpy horror stories. It's what I loved. Still do. My classmates did not. And they let me know it. I was young and lacking in self-esteem and I let them convince me I was a talentless hack; a *Fraud Serling* whose stories should be on *Tales from the Crapped*. (I made the names up, but that was the general gist of it.)

Still, silly goose that I am, I believed that crap for the next quarter of a century. In fact, it wasn't until 2012 that I finally started writing fiction again. (I'm an advertising copywriter for my day job, which some could argue is just another form of fiction, but it pays the bills, and it mostly scratched my creative itch. Mostly.)

Then one Saturday I woke up with the last few lines for "Fresh" in my head. I grabbed a pen and wrote that shit down. The first draft sucked (don't they all?), but the act of writing something original that didn't require a legal disclaimer felt great. I kept at it off and on over the next few years, but it wasn't until a writer's retreat at The Stanley Hotel in 2015 (the setting for my story "The Tunnel at the End of the Light") and my first StokerCon in 2016 that I started to get a little more serious about it.

Countless classes, workshops, bootcamps, writers' groups, conventions, and two appearances on the Preliminary Stoker ballot for Superior Achievement in Short Fiction later, and here we are.

There are so many friends and family who've helped me along the way, and I'm sure I'll forgot some names (please don't hate me!), but in no particular here goes: Julie Crone, Amy Leslie, and Chris Selders, my first beta readers back in the day; the OG Friends of Poe (Rebecca Allred, Mary Ann Back, and Bryan Prince); the Monday Night Write Club (John Buja, Cory Cone, Stephen Cords, Terry Emery, Victoria Fredrick, Ken Godfrey, Jessica McMahan, Valerie Williams, and especially Christa Carmen and her (not so) gentle character whip); Jeff Strand for showing me that horror comedy is a thing; my eternal frenemy Tom Deady; and all the editors and publishers who took a chance on my stories over the years.

Finally, an extra-special thanks to my mom Barbara (they got you way too soon) for introducing me to horror at an entirely way-too-early age; my wife Vanessa, who, despite never reading my stuff (she's not a horror fan), believed in me even when I didn't, which, let's be honest, is still more often than not; and my doggos Koko, for always pushing me toward the Next Big Thing, and Sammie, for all the words. I miss you both dearly and hope you're waiting for me over the Rainbow Bridge.

Larry Hinkle, 6-27-2023

THE DUDE IN THE ORANGE
WOOL HAT

Larry began stalking me in 2015 during a writing retreat at the Stanley Hotel in Estes Park, Colorado. Of course, I didn't know it at the time. Fate, or perhaps some meticulous planning on Larry's part, put us at the same table for the awards banquet in 2016 at StokerCon in Las Vegas. What are the odds? The following year at StokerCon – this one on the Queen Mary in Long Beach, CA - a bunch of us were talking when we realized we'd *all* been at the Stanley for that retreat but hadn't really interacted much. Sure enough, when I went back and looked at pictures from the Stanley, there was Larry in his bright orange wool hat lurking in the background of every photo I took.

We stayed in touch online and he followed me around at conventions a couple times each year, but it wasn't until I joined the Monday Night Write Club that I realized Larry's talent. And I'm not just saying that because he's holding me prisoner in this musty dungeon until I write a foreword for him. I really mean it.

I think it's fitting that the first story in this collection is titled "THAT'S WHAT FRIENDS ARE FOR." Larry is a cool guy, a great husband, avid dog-lover, and a unique writer, but above all, he's a true friend. He told me so himself.

Hopefully most of you don't have friends like the one in Larry's story.

"STRANGE CONSTELLATIONS" highlights Larry's skills at both cosmic horror and coming-of-age horror. A corn maze with shambling creatures and malicious vines reads like a cross between *The Ruins* and *Children of the Corn* with a hint of those creepy, moonlight-drenched woods beyond the deadfall in *Pet Sematary*.

Larry's penchant for the bizarre shines through in "TRASH TALK," as does his sharp wit, when a 90-foot sentient garbage dump terrorizes a town. Only from the mind of Larry Hinkle.

In "SHARING IS CARING," Larry brings the full force of his dark humor forward while giving a nod to some classic horror movie villains.

I had planned to talk about each one of Larry's stories, but the light is getting pretty dim down here and I think I hear footsteps above me. So, I need to hurry things up.

Suffice to say, there is a little something for everyone in this collection. Think of it as a horror buffet where you can sample a little of this and a little of that until you find your taste.

There are holiday stories – Halloween and Christmas will never be the same after you read them. There are stories about cannibalism and necrophilia. There is one that takes place at the legendary Stanley Hotel, written during that writing retreat I mentioned where Larry and I first crossed paths.

Like I said, something for all appetites. Larry's writing spans the gamut of the horror spectrum. Cosmic, the uncanny, coming-of-age, sentient garden gnomes, and yes, even clown horror! It's all in here.

So, come closer, sample a little of what Larry is offering. There's a cruel darkness here, but it's disguised with cunning wit and clever dialogue so you might not see it coming.

Just remember, when you're done, step outside and look to the sky. See those stars? Do you recognize them? Are they *your* stars?

That's all for now. The hour grows late, as they say in the horror stories, and Larry is anxious to read this. I hope he likes it. Because I really want to make him happy.

After all, isn't that what friends are for?

Tom Deady
September 2023
Larry's basement, somewhere in Maryland

THE SPACE BETWEEN

THAT'S WHAT FRIENDS ARE FOR

The plastic seat is hard and cold against my back and thighs. I don't mind, though, because until last week, before I finally changed, I hadn't been able to feel anything from your world. Down the hall, a sickly yellow fluorescent light flickers on and off. I tap my feet against the faded linoleum floor, in time with the heartbeat of the guard hanging around the nurses' station. The tapping's not loud enough for anyone to hear, but the fact I'm making any noise at all makes me smile.

The morning nurse finishes checking on Bobby. When she leaves, she makes a note on the clipboard hanging outside his room, then looks through me as if I weren't even there.

It's okay. I'm used to it. Grown-ups can't see me unless I want them to. And trust me, since my change, you don't want to. Pets and animals can, though, so I have to be careful around them. Especially now. Kids too, but only when they're young. Once they reach a certain age, usually around their 7th or 8th birthday, their ability fades. After that, it's only a matter of time until they forget all about me. "Out of sight, out of mind," as my dad likes to say. Bobby's nurse probably had a friend like me when she was younger.

You did too, I bet. You just don't remember us.

But we remember you.

Bobby just turned seven last month, so I knew the day was coming when he'd forget me. And I knew it was going to hurt. A lot. We'd been best friends since a couple weeks before his first birthday, after all. He'd been able to see me earlier than any other friend I'd had, which is why we were so close. I'd be there when he woke up and stay until he went to sleep. It never mattered to me what we were doing, just that we were doing it together.

His mom would check in on us every now and then, and he'd tell her about the fun we were having. She'd act like she could see me, sure. She'd even make me a little lunch sometimes. But I knew she was faking. Bobby's dad was the same way. He'd come home from work and ask

Bobby about his day. Bobby would tell him about our adventures, and his dad would say how lucky Bobby was to have such a great friend. And then his dad would walk right through me on his way to the kitchen.

It's okay. Like I said, I'm used to it.

Bobby wasn't even the first friend to outgrow me. There were plenty of others before him. My dad says we age slower than you do, and it's normal for us to lose a few friends before the change, although that doesn't make it hurt any less.

Bobby will definitely be the last, though.

***

The day it happened, the day everything changed for both of us, started like any other. I was waiting by Bobby's bed when he woke up, even though I figured he'd ignore me. Heck, we'd barely done anything together since his birthday, thanks to that stupid tablet his grandma gave him. Now all he wanted to do was play games with his new friends online. It wasn't fair. It's not my fault his tablet fell through my hands when he handed it to me. He really should have known better. Lucky for him, it landed on a pillow. I don't know how many times I said I was sorry, but it didn't make a difference.

His parents must have noticed, because one night they asked Bobby about me. He shrugged and kept playing on his tablet. "I guess our little man's growing up," I overheard his mom say later. "He doesn't have time for his invisible friend anymore."

Anyway, I wasn't completely invisible to Bobby yet, so I kept showing up, because that's what friends are for, right? And that morning Bobby actually wanted to play. With me! I was so happy. Things were like they used to be, just me and my best friend, together again. And we played all my favorite games. We explored the magic caves where Bobby and I had our very first adventure. We hunted dinosaurs and tamed a Tyrannosaurus. We named him Ted, after Bobby's weird uncle. We even built a rocket ship and flew to Mars. We invited the Martians to lunch, but Bobby ate his grilled cheese sandwich before they even sat down. I was about to offer them some tomato soup when Bobby grabbed it and slurped it down too. He didn't even ask. So rude. As soon as he finished, he got up and ran back to his room.

I apologized to the Martians and followed Bobby down the hall. When I got to his room, my heart broke. He was back online with his new friends. He hadn't missed me. His tablet had been updating all morning and he'd been bored. Now that it was back up and running, he'd forgotten all about me.

Again.

Dad always told me that someday it'd be my turn to outgrow a friend like the others had outgrown me. "I know it'll hurt, but it has to happen before you can change," he'd say. "But when you come out the other side, you're really gonna boogie, man." You wouldn't know it by looking at him, but my dad has a wicked sense of humor.

I was scared, sure, but a part of me was looking forward to it too. I mean, every boy wants to grow up like his dad, don't they? But as the years went by and more and more friends outgrew me, I started to give up hope. I think Dad did too.

But something inside me snapped that day, seeing Bobby use me like he did. I wasn't just mad at Bobby. I hated his guts! And the only cave I wanted to explore was his abdominal cavity. I kicked at a pillow in frustration. Usually my foot would've gone right through it, but this time the pillow moved. Just a bit, but I felt it. I'd actually touched something!

I was so surprised, I forgot all about being mad. If I could kick a pillow, maybe I could hold Bobby's tablet too. We could still play together! "Hey, Bobby," I yelled. "Did you see that? I kicked the pillow! Watch!"

I tried it again, but this time my foot went right through it, like it usually did. I was so embarrassed.

"Go away," Bobby said. His eyes stayed glued to the screen.

"But…"

"I said get out of here! I don't want to play with you anymore!" He didn't even bother to look up.

My world went red. This time when I kicked the pillow, it flew across the room!

I couldn't believe it. After all these years, was I finally going to change because of Bobby and his stupid tablet?

It didn't take long to find out. My hands tingled as my fingernails lengthened into claws. I ran my tongue over my teeth. There were too many to count, all pointy and sharp. My jaw cracked and widened to make room for them all. The blood on my tongue tasted salty and warm and delicious. The room went blurry, then snapped into focus. Everything was so much clearer now. I could count the hairs on Bobby's head if I wanted to. And the smells! Tomato soup on Bobby's breath, his mom's shampoo, a dead mouse under the deck… I could hear Bobby's heartbeat. His mom's and little sister's too. I could feel muscles rippling under my skin, growing bigger and harder and meaner. It all felt so…*nice*. Better than nice, even.

Bobby finally looked up. I was so big now I had to duck under the ceiling fan. "Let's play," I said, my voice deep and wet like my dad's. I grabbed his tablet and smashed it over his head. The screen shattered, and pieces of glass fell onto the bed. Without thinking, I picked one up and stabbed Bobby in the face. Stabbing him felt even better than changing! I stabbed him again and again and again, only stopping when the glass broke off in his eye.

I stood over him, panting, thinking how proud my dad was going to be, when Bobby's mom ran into the room and screamed. It must have been awful for her, seeing her little boy like that, alone in his bedroom, face bloody and raw, a chunk of glass sticking out of his eye. I can't imagine how she felt.

I felt totally awesome!

She wrapped his head in a towel and called 911. It took her a couple tries, since her hands were slick with blood. In the doorway, Bobby's little sister gaped at me, wide-eyed, and screamed. I winked and slid under the bed.

***

Bobby's been in the hospital for a week now. I'm standing in the doorway watching his parents fuss over him. The doctors say he'll need a few more operations, but he'll live. His dad mumbles something about chicks digging scars.

Nobody laughs.

Bobby won't stop asking for a new tablet, but they say he can't have one until he gets home and they talk about what happened. He keeps telling them I did it. Of course, they don't believe him, even though the doctors can't explain how he stabbed himself in the face so many times without cutting his hands.

When his parents leave, they walk right through me. But this time, Bobby's mom shivers and rubs her hand across the back of her neck. That makes me smile.

I follow them out of the hospital into the parking garage. They don't know I'm sitting in the back seat, but Bobby's mom turns the heater up a few degrees on the drive home.

Bobby should be home from the hospital in a few days. I think I'll hide in the closet until he gets back; sharpen my claws a bit while I wait. When he goes to bed, I'll make sure the closet door is open. Just a crack.

And then I'm going to teach him all sorts of new games after his parents turn out the lights.

After all, isn't that what friends are for?

STRANGE CONSTELLATIONS

We crouched low to the ground, watching the corn.

Thirty minutes earlier, I'd been playing ball with my best friend Doug when I mistimed my jump. The ball sailed over my glove and smacked hard into the door of Joe Thompson's cherry-red Camaro as it cruised down the street. Joe slammed the brakes, then he, Mike, and Big Tom— all seniors—jumped out, cussing up a storm. We dropped our gloves and ran for the woods behind my house. Mike and Big Tom took off after us. Joe hopped back in his Camaro and floored it; a red rocket piloted by a lit stick of dynamite. He was going to circle back around behind the woods and try to cut us off.

A few minutes later, we stumbled out of the trees and onto the road. About fifty yards down from us was Old Bob's farm, proud home of the county's oldest corn maze. Doug took off for the maze first, with me hot on his tail. Mike and Big Tom finally came out of the woods and started up after us.

Doug ran straight into the maze without stopping, but I slowed down in the parking lot. Something about the maze didn't look right. It was a perfect autumn day, without a cloud in the sky, but there was a darkness shimmering in the air high above the corn. It looked like night was pushing through the daytime sky. I swear I could see Orion, Taurus, and the Pleiades shining down! I shook my head, and the sky returned to normal.

I looked back down the road. Mike was gaining on us, but Big Tom had fallen way behind. If we were lucky, we might lose the older boys in the corn. It was a big if, but it was the only shot we had, so I followed Doug into the maze.

Six turns in, I heard Joe slam on his brakes, tires sliding across the gravel lot. Mike and Big Tom had stayed at the entrance, waiting for their orders. "Let's go piggy hunting," Joe said, and the three older boys rushed into the maze. "We're coming for you, piggies!" he yelled.

"Sooey!" Mike and Big Tom answered; then all three burst out laughing.

We panicked and ran deeper into the maze. With each turn, the rows narrowed, the stalks grew tighter and taller. Tassels stuck to our sweaty skin and tangled in our hair; husks slapped at our arms and legs. I could hear the older boys yelling in the distance, but they didn't seem to be getting any closer. Maybe we still had a chance.

After a few more minutes, the path we were on ended in a large clearing in the middle of the maze. "What the hell?" Doug huffed, a few paces ahead of me. "How big is this thing?"

"Stop a second, Doug," I wheezed, wiping sweat from my forehead as I tried to catch my breath.

"Are you crazy? We gotta keep moving."

He started for an open row to our left. I grabbed his arm. "Wait! I think we're okay for a second," I said. "Just listen, those guys aren't anywhere near us." We could hear Mike and Big Tom's voices somewhere far off to our left; Joe sounded even further away to the right.

We crouched down and watched the corn. "Let's wait here a little longer," I whispered. "Maybe they'll get tired and leave." Doug nodded, his eyes wide with fear. I knew he had reason to be afraid. There was a nasty scar above his right eyebrow from a beating Joe and Mike had given him last year for spilling a pop on Joe's shoes. Big Tom hadn't joined their gang yet or the beating would have been a lot worse.

"Mike, where did you go?" Big Tom yelled from somewhere to our right. We could hear him crashing through the stalks.

"Where did *I* go?" Mike, still far to our left, sounded pissed. "Where the hell did *you* go?"

"I didn't go anywhere, numbnuts! I just turned around and you were gone."

"Well, stay there," Mike yelled back. "I'm coming over to where you are. And then we're getting out of here. I'm tired of running around looking for those punks."

"But what about Joe?"

"What about him? If he wants to chase his tail in this stupid maze, let him."

"Okay," Big Tom shouted. "But hurry up. It's getting really dark." Was that fear in his voice? I couldn't imagine Big Tom being scared of anything.

"He's right," Doug whispered. "It *is* getting really dark. How long have we been in here?"

I looked up. The sky was the color of an angry bruise, and the stars were coming out. How long *had* we been in the maze? A blood-red moon drifted into view over the edge of the clearing. A second, smaller moon came chasing a few moments later.

"Do you see that?" I whispered.

"What the hell? How are there two moons?"

"It's gotta be a trick," I said. "Maybe the light's bouncing off the clouds or something…"

"Billy, look at all the stars." Doug's voice sounded small and lost.

I held up my hand to block out the moons. Millions of multicolored stars shimmered overhead, way more than should be visible under *one* moon, let alone two. The sky was ablaze with twinkling lights, so many they made me dizzy. But they weren't *my* stars, the ones my dad taught me when I was younger. The constellations were strange, the patterns all jumbled up.

The maze looked like another world in the crimson moonlight. The rows of corn looked different too, the stalks leaning and bending at impossible angles. The colors were harder, more vibrant. It made my eyes ache to look at anything too long. My teeth felt like I was chewing on tin foil.

The air was hot, thick, heavy. Its weight pushed down on us, holding us in place. Every breath was harder than the last. Everything felt *wrong* in a way I couldn't describe. I only knew we didn't belong there, under that alien sky. Nobody did.

The wind picked up. The rustling of the corn sounded like whispering, but in a language I didn't want to understand. The harder the wind blew, the louder the whispering grew, until the cornhusks peeled open and each kernel was a screaming mouth and the sound felt like a dentist's drill in the base of my skull.

From somewhere in the maze, something that *almost* sounded like Joe taunted us. "You don't have to worry about *me* now, piggies!" the thing-that-wasn't-Joe cackled. He started to sing in a high-pitched, childish voice. Mike and Big Tom sang along with him, and soon they were joined by a chorus of voices that seemed to swirl through the rows around the clearing coming from everywhere and nowhere at once and we fell to our knees and covered our ears but our hands couldn't shut out their song and we screamed and screamed and begged for it to end and then everything just…stopped.

I don't know how long we laid there, huddled in the dirt. I'd lost any sense of time and place. But when I felt the earth breathing beneath me— *up and down, up and down*—I knew we had to move.

I shook Doug's shoulder. "Doug, get up. We have to go."

Doug didn't answer. He was curled into a ball, shaking.

In the corn off to our right, I heard someone—some*thing*—moving. I looked up and saw an immense shaggy form in the distance. It towered over the maze as it shambled through the rows. Its eyes blazed a hungry shade of orange.

I shook Doug again, harder this time.

"Doug! We have to go. Now!"

New shoots wiggled up from the soil, swaying in time to an inner music. I knew if I heard the song it would drive me insane. Their blooms opened and released a sickly sweet stench, like the slaughterhouse outside of town on a hot, humid day. I felt something wet on my face and ran my hand across my lip. My nose was bleeding.

Doug finally stood up, panting. The front of his shorts was dark; he'd wet himself. "It's not real it's not real it's not real..." he shouted, over and over again. His eyes were squeezed shut and he had his hands over his ears. The blooms turned at the sound of his voice. New vines snaked up from the dirt and slithered toward us.

The ground pitched violently. Stalks exploded up into the sky. Something was coming. Something *big*.

"Run!" I screamed. I shoved Doug ahead of me and we burst back into the maze. We ran blindly, not paying attention to the path, smashing through walls of corn. The shoots followed us, wriggling over and through the crushed stalks. One of them caught my ankle and wrapped tight, right above my shoe. I screamed in pain and fell down into the dirt. Doug kept going. The ground was teeming with fat, gelatinous, squirming *things* that crawled over my hands and arms, making their way toward my face. I wanted to scream again, but I was afraid to open my mouth. I tried to run, but the vine still had hold of my ankle. I kicked my foot back and forth until I pulled free. My ankle burned where the vine had touched it, and my shoe was wet with blood.

I saw Doug up ahead, skidding and turning down a row to his left. Behind me, I heard Doug scream. *That can't be right*, I thought, *Doug was right up ahead of me*. The scream must have come from one of the older boys.

I turned down the path Doug took and smashed into Big Tom's chest. The impact knocked me back onto my ass. "Jesus, watch where you're going, idiot!" Big Tom said. His voice sounded wet. I looked up at him and screamed. The skin of his face hung down around his collar. His eyes were impossibly white and large against the glistening red meat. His lipless mouth stretched into a toothy grin too wide for his face. "I'm on my way to join the others on the trail," he said. "You're coming too. But first I have to take off your mask." He raked at my cheek, but I ducked out of the way. With all the strength I could muster, I kicked him between the legs and ran. Behind me, Big Tom laughed. His voice grew deeper and gravellier, as if his mouth were full of dirt. "We'll see you soon enough, piggy! All rows lead to the Eris Ridge Trail!"

I shouted for Doug as I ran blindly through the maze. Once, I thought I heard him answer from some place far ahead, but his voice was drowned out by the sound of the shambling beast that patrolled the corn. I kept running, following the path when the rows were clear, smashing through the stalks when they weren't. My own voice was little more than a rasp now. The pain in my legs and lungs felt like I'd been running for hours, but I had no idea how long I'd been trapped there. Or how many times I'd missed the exit.

I turned another blind corner and saw Doug ahead of me, running down a dead-end row. "Doug, wait!" I tried to yell, but my voice was completely gone now. He plowed through the wall of corn and disappeared into the darkness.

I ran after him, trying to catch up. I burst through the row and stumbled into a dusty parking lot. The sunlight blinded me. Holding my hand over my eyes, I heard children playing nearby. I squinted and looked around. I was out of the maze!

Doug was waiting for me about ten feet away. "Can you believe we finally made it out of there?" he asked, laughing in relief. His face was filthy and he had corn tassels in his hair. He patted his chest, and dust puffed off his green t-shirt. His jeans were covered in dirt, and they were totally dry.

Old Bob marched across the parking lot toward us, shaking his finger. "What are you boys doing in my corn? Is that your car?" He pointed to a white Mustang parked in the lot, with a baseball-sized dent above the rear tire. There was at least three days' worth of dust on it.

I shook my head.

"You know whose it is?"

Doug looked at the old man. "Nope, never seen it before," he said. "Have we, Bill?" Doug turned and winked at me. His smile was impossibly wide, and his eyes were black pools. The scar above his eyebrow was gone.

I heard a rustling in the corn behind me. I looked back. There was a darkness in the air high above the maze, and I could see an ocean of stars glittering through the shadow.

But they weren't my stars.

FRESH

Jasper Hossenfeld couldn't leave the bathroom.

He'd washed his hands three times, as always. Dried his hands, two paper towels per hand, as always. Unfortunately, those were the last paper towels in the room. Hell, Jasper wouldn't be surprised if they were the last paper towels in the entire building, from the looks of it. So how was he supposed to open the door now? Without some sort of protection, he certainly wasn't going to touch the handle. A door handle in a dive bar bathroom. Who knows what kind of filth was on it. What kind of filth had *touched* it. After doing God only knows what to themselves. Or their sister. This *was* the backwoods of Kentucky, after all. And Jesus Christ, was that actually a condom dispenser on the wall? With something called *'ticklers'*? This place served food! Well, maybe. Jasper smelled something that others might consider to be food, but it was certainly nothing he'd ever eat.

On the advice of his therapist, Jasper always carried a packet of tissues in his pocket for occasions such as this, along with a bottle of Xanax. But for some reason, tonight his pockets were empty. Even his wallet was gone.

As the muffled stylings of Hank Williams carried through the door, Jasper turned back to look at himself in the mirror. Not only were his pockets empty, they weren't even his pockets! What happened to the clothes he'd been wearing when he'd left the house that morning? He had a long drive to a meeting the next day, and he'd dressed for the drive—loose fitting chinos (with deep pockets) and a V-neck grey cotton t-shirt. Casual. Comfortable. Nondescript. He'd even made a few sandwiches for the trip—free-range chicken, homemade mayo from cage-free eggs, lettuce and tomatoes he'd grown from carefully selected heirloom seeds, seven-grain stone-ground wheat bread—all hermetically sealed and packed on ice so there was no chance of germs or contamination.

Now he was wearing a Slayer t-shirt with red paint splashed across the front. And his pants were tight black jeans that left *very* little to the imagination.

What the fuck was going on here?

He remembered driving, reaching for a sandwich, a flash of light, and then he was here. Everything in between was gone. Had he been in an accident of some sort? He didn't seem hurt. No broken bones, no bruises, not even a scratch that he could see. But where was his car? Why was he here, instead of a hospital? And goddammit, where were his clothes?

Shit! Jasper's thoughts were starting to spiral. He could ask for help when he got out of the bathroom, but without his tissues, that wasn't happening anytime soon. He couldn't just grab the paper towels from the trashcan; he'd get his hands dirty. Again. And then he'd have to wash. Again. And he still wouldn't be any closer to opening the door. He was trapped. Fucking OCD. What was he going to do?

A knock on the door interrupted his thoughts.

"Jasper, buddy, how you doing in there? You okay?"

Redemption.

Or was it? Jasper had no idea who was on the other side of the door, or how they knew his name. He didn't recognize their voice. And none of his friends would ever bring him to a place like this. Right. Like he had any friends. His numerous mental tics made it near impossible for him to relate to other people on anything but the most superficial of levels. Sure, he got along okay with his coworkers, but that was mainly because they knew enough to leave him alone and let him do his job. After all, his tics made them money. And that, in turn, made it easier for them to put up with him. He didn't mind though. Not really. Not having friends meant not having to rely on anyone else.

Until now, of course.

Still, if the person on the other side of the door knew his name, they must know what happened to him, right? Which meant Jasper would just have to suck it up and trust him. At least long enough to figure a way out of this jam.

"The door's stuck," Jasper said. "I can't open it."

The handle turned and the door swung open. A policeman stepped aside to let Jasper out. "Seemed to open okay for me," he said.

"Thanks, Officer. Now maybe you can tell me what the hell is going on here."

***

"This is ridiculous."

"What?" asked the policeman.

"This!" hissed Jasper. "Jesus, I'm an economics strategist, not a criminal."

"Never said you were," the cop answered with the slightest shrug of his tired shoulders. "Just said I didn't like the way you were driving."

"So why are we here, at some dive bar…"

"Roadhouse," the cop said, correcting Jasper. "This, Jasper, is a roadhouse."

The policeman waved his arm to prove his point that this was, indeed, a roadhouse. Bikers gathered by the pool tables, cracked, worn paneling with names and dates scratched in it to commemorate conquests best forgotten, tables buried under mounds of fried food and pitchers of beer, smoke swirling round the lights like fog round the Golden Gate Bridge, waitresses with tramp stamps the size of which are rarely seen outside of low-rent strip clubs.

"Okay, it's a roadhouse. But that doesn't explain why we're here, drinking tequila. I'm not even supposed to be drinking *caffeine* with the meds I'm on," Jasper said, before nervously sniffing his shot. "And I'm certainly not going to be driving any better after this."

"Like I said, you weren't driving all that well to begin with, buddy. Maybe you should try to eat something."

Jasper's stomach came alive at the mention of food. He remembered making his special sandwiches earlier in the day, but he couldn't remember eating them. Or even where they were now. Which meant he hadn't eaten since breakfast. Not good. He had a very strict schedule he needed to stick to in order to balance out his meds. That's probably why the alcohol was going to his head so fast. At least he assumed it was the alcohol, since he didn't drink and therefore had nothing to compare the feeling to. Everything just seemed a little *off* to Jasper right now though. The lights were brighter, the music louder, even the smells were more intense. He wouldn't have thought it possible, but he felt even more *different* now than he normally did, like he was vibrating at a slightly higher frequency than everything around him.

As hungry as he was, however, the thought of eating at a bar—scratch that, *roadhouse*—killed his appetite. The cop could throw him in jail for DUI if he wanted, but there was no way in hell Jasper was going to eat anything made in a place like this.

"Eat something? Here?" Jasper was stunned the cop had the audacity to even suggest such a thing. "What are you, crazy? It's bad enough you're making me drink with you, but you're out of your mind if you expect me to eat here. I don't eat anything that isn't fresh and that I haven't made myself. Period."

To emphasize his point, Jasper picked up a menu and shoved it at the officer. "You think these wings come from free-range chickens? No. And I guarantee the onions in these rings are *not* organic. Nor are the potatoes in these fries. Jesus, they don't even offer a gluten-free bun for their burgers." He tossed the menu back down on the bar and pointed toward the kitchen. "And who knows what kind of germs these Neanderthals are breeding in that 'kitchen' of theirs. At least the alcohol should sterilize my glass."

"Don't worry about it, then," said the cop. "I'll drive."

"Drive where?"

"I'm taking you to school, Jasper."

"Excuse me?"

"Yeah, you and me, we're chaperoning the prom. Call it public service if you want. But you need to drink up, friend. That county's dry."

***

Jasper slammed his shot glass down on the bar. "Six!" he shouted to nobody in particular. Which was fitting, as nobody in particular was paying him any attention. "Six," he said again, more softly.

"Six," echoed the cop. "You know, that used to be my number, back in the day."

"Your number was six?" asked Jasper. "What, were you an athlete or something?"

The police officer put down his empty glass and turned to Jasper.

"I bet you only asked me that because I'm black, didn't you?"

"No, because I'm half-drunk. Or at least what I assume being half-drunk feels like, since, as I'm sure I've mentioned to you at least a couple times tonight, I don't drink anything stronger than sparkling water." He paused. "Besides, cops don't have numbers, do they? Other than your badge number, I mean."

"No, but angels do."

"Angels? I knew it! You used to play baseball, didn't you? What position? Pitcher? Catcher? Shortstop?"

"Hardly," the cop answered before signaling for another round. "But I have played, Jasper. Oh, how I've played."

***

Staring into his shot glass, the police officer took a moment to reflect on his playing days, before everything went to shit. That whole "angel of light" thing was supposed to be a joke. But the Big Guy took it the wrong way, and the next thing you know, his wings were gone and he'd been banished to this cesspool. Where he sat with his latest disciple.

Jasper.

Anal-retentive, OCD Jasper. Jasper, whose car four hours prior had drifted left-of-center before being broadsided by a delivery truck.

Of course, poor Jasper had fared better than the driver who'd hit him.

It was really too bad the driver had approached the car during Jasper's "rescue." Too bad he'd seen the policeman pull Jasper from the wreckage and remove his torn and bloody clothing. Too bad he'd seen him lick Jasper's wounds, then gently kiss him on the mouth. Too bad he'd seen Jasper then rise and pose, perfectly flexible, like a mannequin, as the policeman dressed him in new clothes. And *way* too bad that he ran back to call someone on his radio.

If not for that last move, the policeman might have let him live. Let the driver try explaining *that* to all his friends at work. But he couldn't have word of Jasper's resurrection hitting the airwaves. Not yet, at least. So he just *had* to let Jasper tear out the driver's throat. Didn't have a choice, really. Good for Jasper, since he needed to feed, but bad for his favorite Slayer shirt. Reign in blood, indeed.

Truth be told, he wasn't even looking for a partner. But the opportunity was just too good to pass up. At least, it had seemed that way when he'd come across the wreck. Now, after spending a couple hours with Jasper, he wasn't so sure. His newest disciple dressed like a Gap model, had more personality quirks than Carter had liver pills, and couldn't even manage to extricate himself from a roadhouse bathroom.

Jesus. Over the centuries, his quality of help had certainly diminished. And with it, his ambition. Or was it the other way around? Like attracts like, as they say. As who says? He didn't remember anymore. Of course, there were a lot of things he didn't remember anymore. Probably a result of being on his own for such a long, long time. Sure, he'd had companions over the years, but they tended not to last too long. Humans just weren't cut out for this line of work, even after he removed their humanity.

Not their fault, really. In the end, they were only monkeys. Monkeys with free will. And the souls that went along with it. He never understood why they'd been given such a gift. He understood even less why they continued to squander it. After all this time, they still squabbled over the silliest things. Imaginary borders. Religion. Sex. Drugs. Rock and roll. They were never, ever happy, because they had no idea how much they really had.

Still, they did invent tequila, so he couldn't complain too much.

He checked his watch, tossed back his shot, and threw some money at the bartender. "Grab your stuff, Jasper. We don't wanna be late for the King and Queen ceremony."

***

At this point in the evening, to say Jasper had a bad feeling about his companion would be an insult to bad feelings. Jasper had a very, *very* bad feeling about this guy. For one thing, he drank. A lot. For another, he didn't seem to breathe. Ever. His courage bolstered by the alcohol, Jasper decided to risk a personal question. "So, you're not really a cop, are you?"

"What makes you say that? The fact that we didn't stop at any donut shops since we got back on the road?"

"No, it was pretty much your lack of breathing."

"Jasper, my boy," the cop chuckled, "you're not as stupid as I thought. But there is one thing you seem to have overlooked."

"What's that?"

"You're not breathing either."

Jasper gasped. Well, it was really more of a breathless reflex, since in order to gasp, one needs to possess the ability to inhale, something Jasper had lost earlier that evening.

His head was spinning. "Where are my clothes?" he asked, his voice gaining rapidly in both speed and volume. "Where's my car? Who are you? What the fuck did you do to me?"

At first, the cop didn't even look at Jasper. But after pulling to a stop at the far end of the school parking lot, he turned and smiled, his eyes twinkling in the reflection of the red and blue strobes blinking from atop the cruiser. As Jasper watched, they became empty holes, a bottomless black so deep Jasper imagined if he fell into them, he'd never escape. The officer blinked, and his eyes returned to normal. "All in good time, Jasper, all in good time."

He put the car in park and killed the engine.

"I promise, as soon as we're done here, I'll tell you everything, okay? But right now, I need you to focus. There's going to be an…incident…at the prom in a few minutes, and we have to be there to take care of it."

"But, my car…" Jasper said, his voice trailing off. "My clothes…"

"Like I said, Jasper, all in good time. Let's just get through this, you and me, and we'll get everything sorted out after that, okay?"

Jasper hesitated. "Okay," he agreed, finally. "But you promise you're going to tell me everything when this is done, right? And I mean everything."

"Sure, Jasper, I'll tell you whatever you want to know. Now come on."

The policeman turned off the lights and exited the vehicle. Was he bigger now, or was it just a trick of the parking lot lights? Jasper got out of the car, and together they started walking toward the school entrance. Through the windows, they could hear sounds of the prom, now in full swing. Laughter. Music. Singing. Teens on the cusp of adulthood, enjoying a night ablaze with anticipation and promise. Innocent souls without the slightest inkling of the hell that was coming for them.

Outside the door, the policeman stopped, turned, and looked down at Jasper. "Hey, Jasper, just do me a favor, okay?"

Looking up at the police officer—had he really grown another foot taller?—Jasper didn't answer.

The policeman, however, didn't seem to mind. "Once we get started, try not to scream."

***

The science programs Jasper liked to watch said time slowed down for people during moments of extreme duress: your senses were heightened, your memories enhanced, as your brain processed gigabytes of extra information and observations. In real life, at least for Jasper, the exact opposite happened. In fact, he couldn't believe how quickly the slaughter took place, and could barely remember his part in it. One minute he and the policeman were walking into the gym (the policeman ducking beneath the school's eight-foot doorframe); the very next, it seemed, they were walking back out toward the car.

Jasper stumbled and fell forward. The policeman caught him and helped him lean back against the car. Jasper thanked the officer, who'd somehow returned to his normal size, then turned and watched the school burn.

He coughed, a violent convulsion that filled his mouth with a ball of coppery soot and ash. The mixture made Jasper's stomach lurch, and he bent over to spit out the toxic phlegm. And as he rested there, hands on knees, head hanging down, he began to remember...

He remembered driving. Reaching for a sandwich. A flash of light. He remembered the truck hitting his car, flipping it over and knocking it off the road. Then, nothing.

Wait. He remembered...*the other driver, running back toward his truck. Jasper jumping toward the driver, Jasper jumping* over *the driver, landing between his killer and the safety of the cab. He remembered the sound of someone on the radio asking if the driver was okay. He remembered the hunger. He remembered...feeding. His mind went red.*

The police officer shook Jasper's shoulder. "Hey, Jasper, you okay?"

Jasper looked up at the officer and cocked his head. "I'm...fine," he said, standing back up and staring into the fire. The officer nodded, and Jasper's world turned crimson.

He remembered his "awakening" in the bathroom. Their time together at the bar. The drive to the school. Walking into the school. Seeing all the young sucklings gathered together, looking up at the stage, where their new King and Queen had just been crowned. Poor meatsacks. They had no idea what a true *King was. But Jasper would show them. Jasper* did *show them. As the police officer quietly locked the doors, Jasper leapt to the stage and removed the King's crown from his head, before removing the King's head from his body. He wore them both as a hat. He sliced at the Queen, opening her jugular. He drank.*

He remembered telling the police officer he could have the stoners and the drunks, he was disgusted by the smell of their fermented blood. He wanted nothing to do with the athletes, their muscles and organs drowning in steroids and human growth hormone. He also refused the girls he considered "unclean," those menstruating or promiscuous or both.

The wallflowers and the geeks and the freaks and the nerds and the loners, however, were his. Jasper knew these people. Jasper was one of these people. Had been his entire life.

These people were pure.

They were untouched.

They were fresh.

And they were his.

Oh God, were they his. For he was their King, and they were his new reason for living. They were his bread. His butter. His goddamn turkey, stuffing, and green bean casserole, all rolled into one big Hallelujah. They were his life. And he, theirs. At least for the few minutes they had left to live.

A tap on his shoulder brought him back to reality.

It was the police officer. His maker. His...friend. "We need to get going, Jasper," his new friend said. "The real authorities will be here soon." He watched as his friend opened the driver's door and settled in behind the wheel. Jasper couldn't believe his luck—a friend! He hoped they'd be able to play together forever.

Before opening the door, Jasper allowed himself one last look back toward the school. Correction: toward where the school *used* to be. Now, there was just fire. And smoke. And ash.

There was also blood.

Blood, dripping from his fingers.

From his hair.

From his clothes.

Some was his.

Most was not.

"Fresh," he whispered, chewing at a stringy piece of the Queen's flesh buried under the nail of his index finger.

Just the way he liked it.

TRASH TALK

"What do you think the worst thing about fighting a ninety-foot sentient garbage creature would be? I mean, apart from its impenetrable concrete and metal outer skin." I look at the old man and the two younger men with him I've dubbed the Mustaches. Are they coworkers? Father and sons? A throuple? Enquiring minds want to know.

"It's gotta be the stink, right? I mean, we can smell it all the way up here." I wave my hand in front of my nose.

One of them, Mustache Two maybe, grunts in response. The old man clears his throat and spits over the edge of the cliff. Just my luck to run into an apocalyptic trio of Silent Bobs.

The three of them were already parked on top of the mesa when I'd pulled up. Now we're watching the garbage creature destroy what's left of our town below. The army had ordered us to evacuate two days ago. The only people still in town are military, first responders, and rednecks with a hard-on for blowing shit up. We think we're safe up here, but our trucks are idling in case we need to make a quick exit.

"But where does the smell come from?" I ask. I'm not about to let their lack of interest slow me down. "I mean, aside from the dirty diapers and rotting food. Trash water, that's my bet." They look at me, slack-jawed. "You know, that bit of liquid that accumulates at the bottom of your garbage can? Even when there's nothing wet in the bag, somehow the can still has a stinky, sloshy puddle in the bottom? Yeah, that stuff."

The old man rolls his eyes. I can tell he already regrets waving me over. Whatever. I know I get on people's nerves. Hell, ADHD meant I had a hard time with silence *before* this shit started. And it certainly didn't help that the soldiers who evacuated our block rushed me out of the house before I could grab my Adderall. But seriously, how can anyone not want to talk about it? It's a living landfill, for Christ's sake.

And people say nothing cool ever happens around here.

A power transformer explodes somewhere below us. "Twenty bucks says that thing sweats trash water." I point toward the creature. "Or pisses it everywhere. Kinda like how rats are constantly peeing because they don't have bladders."

"That's not true," Mustache One says.

Hallelujah! At least one of them isn't a deaf mute.

"Course it is," I counter. "Everyone knows rats don't have bladders."

"Rats do so have bladders," Mustache Two says. "I'll grant you they pee a lot, but they most definitely have bladders."

We duck as two fighter jets scream overhead.

"Fellas, I think we're getting off track here," I say once we can hear each other again. I can't stop now. The words are coming almost faster than I can process them. "I'm just saying that thing is probably oozing trash water, or spraying it out its pores like a fine mist everywhere it goes. I feel bad for the soldiers down there, man. Their uniforms have to be soaked with the stuff. They better watch they don't get trench foot."

The old man looks at me in either disbelief or disgust. Maybe both.

"Shit, I bet we've lost as many people to the stench as the actual battle," I say. "We're way up here and it's all I can do to keep from tossing my cookies. Can you imagine trying to aim at something when you got puke spraying out your nose?"

"Maybe the army should toss a few 55-gallon drums of Axe body spray at it," Mustache One says.

"That's not a bad idea," Mustache Two says. "But which scent?"

"Apollo?" Mustache One suggests.

"Too much sage," Mustache Two counters. "What about Phoenix?"

Mustache One strokes his mustache. "A subtle combination of mint and rosemary. I like it."

I'm losing control of the conversation. Time to rein 'em back in. "Fellas, I love Axe as much as the next horny single dude, but trust me, the chemicals that gave life to that thing would just neutralize whichever scent you picked."

"How do you know chemicals brought it to life?" The old man's eyes narrow.

Fuck.

I shrug. "Lucky guess?"

I can tell by the look he gives me he isn't buying it. Neither are the Mustaches, who are actually much bigger and burlier than I first thought.

I throw up my hands and start backing toward my truck. "Okay, look, all I'm gonna say is a friend of mine may or may not have been responsible for some illegal barrels that may or may not have found their way into the dump that may or may not have helped bring that thing to life. Allegedly."

The old man's eyes widen. "A *friend*, huh?"

I never see the punch coming.

***

I wake up in a makeshift interrogation room, one wrist handcuffed to the table. I know it's not the police station, because I'd watched the creature smash that entire block on the news.

A grizzled military man stands across from me. Buzz cut, stubbled cheeks. Dried blood marks a nasty gash across his forehead. His uniform is dirty and torn, but I count four stars. *A general*, I think, *great*. Overseeing general disarray from the looks of it. *Don't say it*, I tell myself. I bite my cheek until the urge passes.

"So I hear you're the fucknut responsible for this mess?" the general asks, gesturing to a TV cart in the corner. A TV/VCR combo like we used to have in high school is tuned to one of the news channels. The sound is off, but I don't need to hear what's happening to know things are bad.

On screen is live footage from a helicopter circling the creature at what they must think is a safe distance. "What the fuck are they doing?" the general yells, pointing at the screen. He turns to a soldier standing by the door. "Tell them to get the hell out of there!" The soldier runs out of the room to relay the order.

Even on a crap TV like this, the garbage monster is still scary as fuck. Ninety feet of rubble in the shape of a man, like a Transformer made from the shit we throw away. On the ground, tanks are firing, but the explosions have no effect on the creature. A fighter jet gets too close, and the monster swats it out of the sky. The pilot ejects about three seconds before his jet smashes into the ground. Too late.

As we watch, the creature snatches a water tower off the roof of a building. Then, faster than a giant pile of garbage has any right to move, it turns and flings the tower at the helicopter.

The screen goes black.

The general turns toward me, his face redder than a baboon's ass.

I hold up my free hand. "Okay, I'll admit, that looks bad, but in my defense, how was I supposed to know something like this was going to happen? Sure, maybe if I'd paid more attention in chemistry class, I might have had an inkling. But scientists still don't know for sure what chemicals made up the so-called primordial stew."

"Don't you mean soup?" he asks.

"What?"

"I'd always heard it described as primordial soup."

I shrug. "Tomato, tomahto. Like I said, I didn't pay much attention."

"Gee, thanks, Madame Curie. Now why don't you tell us how this happened?" The general leans over the table. If he's trying to intimidate me, it's working. I can't let him know it though.

"Between you and me, I don't know what was in the barrels I've been dumping there," I say, locking eyes. "It's not like they had 'Danger—Primordial Soup and/or Stew' stickers on them. Although that would definitely have been helpful." I glance at the MP standing behind me. "Hey, when this is over, someone should look into that. Maybe you should write our congressman. Or do we have a congresswoman? Congressperson? Whatever. Might be a commendation in it for you."

He punches me in the nose.

"*Fuck!*" I rub my finger under my nose to make sure it isn't bleeding, then wipe the tears from my eyes. "That's one," I say, hoping I sound braver than I feel.

I take a moment to collect my thoughts. "Look, General Dis—" I stop myself right before *Disarray* slips out. I'm in deep enough shit as it is. "General, sir, I was told to dump them, so I dumped them. Maybe I shouldn't have been so literal and tried disposing of them in the woods instead of an actual dump, but hindsight being 20/20, that's just picking nits, isn't it?"

The MP smacks the back of my head.

I turn and stare at him. "Seriously? That's two." *Jesus, why did I start counting?* I think.

I take a deep breath, then return my attention to the general. "Anyway, there were storms in the forecast when I picked up that night's load. I could see lightning flashes over the horizon as I drove toward the dump. I didn't mind. Figured it would help cover any noise I might make breaking in. It's not like the dump had a lot of security. Just a padlock and a couple strands of barbed wire strung along the top of the fence." I lean forward. "You know, as long as we're pointing fingers, maybe you should start with the person in charge of that? I'm just saying…"

The general nods toward the MP, who smacks me again.

I rub the back of my head. "That's three," I say, not bothering to turn around this time. His snicker tells me he isn't buying my tough guy schtick.

The general cocks his chin. "You were saying…?"

"I was saying, I snipped the lock, drove my truck in, then shut the gate behind me in case anyone came nosing around. Drove to my usual spot near the back of the dump, next to a 'No Hazardous Materials

Allowed' sign. The way I figured it, why would anyone look for hazardous materials in a place where they clearly weren't supposed to be, right?"

The general lowers his head and massages his temples.

"I dropped the tailgate, set up my ramp, and started rolling the barrels down. A gust of wind almost blew me out of the truck and I lost control of a barrel. The top came off when it hit the ground, and some kind of goop oozed out. It was glowing iridescent green, like that snot monster from *Ghostbusters*. I kicked the next barrel down the ramp, and of course it hit the spilled barrel and its top came off too.

"I couldn't tell what color this goop was, on account of it started to smoke as soon as it hit the green stuff. I stood there trying to decide my next move when *ZAP!*" I smack the table for emphasis. "A bolt of lightning hit a piece of metal sticking out of the pile about twenty yards away.

"There was electricity in the air, obviously, but now there was something else too. Something *moaned* inside the pile, which isn't the right word, but I don't how else to describe it, and then the garbage started shifting. I figured the lightning must have knocked something loose in there, and since I didn't want to get buried under a garbage avalanche—ooh, would that be a garbalanche? Or maybe a trashalanche—"

The general slams his fist onto the table. I snap back to attention. "Sorry, since I didn't want to get buried in a garbalanche, I rolled the last barrel out, threw the ramp in the back of the truck, and took off.

"Another bolt of lightning lit up the night as I drove away, and for a second I thought I saw something silhouetted against the sky in my rearview. I figured it was just a trick of the light and forgot all about it until I turned on the news the next morning and saw a giant garbage creature was tearing its way through town."

"Is there anyone who might know what was in those barrels?" the general asks.

"My boss. He called that morning. Woke me up, actually. Pissed me off because he knew I was working late the night before dumping his stupid barrels. That's management for ya. No respect for the little guy." I wince, waiting for the smack. When it doesn't come, I keep talking. "I kept my mouth shut though, because he sounded even more pissed than I was. Wanted to know if I had anything to do with this. More importantly, he wanted to know if I'd done anything they could trace back to him. The way he asked made me think he already knew the answer to that question, so I decided to tell the truth."

"Which was?"

"I told him he was breaking up and ended the call. It wasn't long after that your soldiers came and evacuated my neighborhood. They owe me a bottle of Adderall, by the way."

The general asks for my boss' name and address. He taps a few keys on his laptop, then turns it toward me. "This where he lived?" On the screen is a satellite view of the boss' house. It's been flattened.

"Can you enhance that?" I ask, ducking before the MP can hit me again. Instead, he grabs my head and bounces my face off the table.

"Enhance *that*," the MP says.

There's a pool of dark blood on the table when I lift my head. My nose is bent sideways and my eye is already swelling shut. I run my forearm across my lips to wipe the blood from my mouth.

"That's *four*," the general says. He waits, daring me to make a move. We both know I'm not going to.

But something is tickling the back of my brain. What did it mean that the garbage monster flattened my boss' house? Was that a coincidence? It had to be, didn't it? Otherwise, that meant the garbage monster is smart. And if it's smart… The tickle turns into someone pounding my brain like a speed bag.

The general pokes me in the forehead. "I can almost hear the gears turning in there, Einstein." I snatch at his finger, grabbing a handful of air. "Or should I call you Frankenstein? Because in case you haven't figured it out yet, we believe the creature is looking for you and your boss. Which is why we're delivering you on a silver platter."

My stomach drops.

He picks up his helmet and walks toward the door. "Throw him on the truck," he tells the MP.

I never see that punch coming either.

***

I wake up having no idea how long I've been out. I'm tied up on the back of a flatbed truck parked on an abandoned airstrip outside of town. I feel like Fay Wray in *King Kong*: bait for the monster. At least they didn't dress me in a coconut bikini. My boss is tied up next to me, unconscious, I hope. Guess he wasn't home when the monster crushed his house. Lucky him. Too bad about his face, though. Looks like he hasn't been as cooperative as I have.

Parked next to the truck is an Army Jeep. The general and a few other soldiers are studying a map spread across the hood. Two of the soldiers look like they drove through a car wash with the top down. I knew it—trash water! I'm just glad my nose is too swollen to smell anything. The general shoots me a look that totally cockblocks the giggle building in my chest.

The MP who knocked me out is sitting on a folding chair a few feet away from the post they have us tied to, his back toward us. He's watching the news on a tablet. If I tilt my head just right, I can see about three-quarters of the screen. A reporter is doing a live remote near the remains of City Hall. The general's not gonna like that.

"Hey, can you turn that up?" I ask. The MP flips me the bird, then turns the volume up so I can hear it.

"Scientists still don't know how the garbage became sentient," the reporter says.

"Do they have any clues?" the anchor asks from the safety of a control room two time zones away.

"They're very interested in several chemical barrels they can see in the creature's body."

"What kind of chemicals?"

"The kind that clearly didn't belong in the dump."

"How do they know that?"

"Because there were signs that said 'No Hazardous Materials Allowed' hung near where the military believes the creature became animate. Also, they have security footage of an unidentified man dumping the barrels from the back of his truck. The city installed the cameras after a series of recent break-ins."

Oops.

"You can turn it down now," I say. The MP flips me the bird again.

"Get 'em ready," the general yells. "We're rolling in five."

The MP turns off the tablet. He hands his chair down to another soldier, then checks our bindings. Satisfied we can't pull a Houdini, he jumps off the truck and walks to the cab.

I turn to the Jeep. "Hey, General Disarray," I yell. No point in holding back now. The general looks up at me, his face so red this time it looks like a baboon's ass after a good spanking. I can't help but smile despite my situation. "You really think that thing is looking for us?" I nod toward my boss, who's still not moving.

"Maybe, maybe not. Worth a shot though. Nothing we've done has slowed it down, and we've thrown a lot at it. If this doesn't work, president's deciding whether to hit it with a MOAB or tactical nuke next." He laughs. "Can you believe that? A nuke, on our own soil, and it might not even help. Shit, for all we know, you may have created a new god."

It's his turn to smile now. It doesn't reach his eyes.

"And every god needs a sacrifice."

LOOP DE LOOP DE LOOP

I waited for the machine to power down.

"How will we know if it worked?" I asked.

"If we did our job right, we won't," he said.

"Why?"

He finished his calculations and activated the machine.

"It's Time Travel 101," he said. "If you change something in the past, people in the present won't know it. They can't. Changing a past event changes the path that led to their present, so the need to change the past never existed in the first place."

I waited for the machine to power down.

"How will we know if it worked?" I asked.

REACHING BOTTOM

Kevin's plan is pretty simple. Get to the quarry before dawn. Row out to the middle. Zip tie the heavy chain to his belt loops. Watch the sun rise one last time. Jump.

The summers he spent at the quarry as a teen with his friends were the happiest of his life. It only seems fitting to end it here, to bring things full circle.

The surrounding woods are silent in anticipation of the dawn. The only sound, his paddle dipping beneath the water's surface. Even the fish are quiet this morning. The water smells clean, the scent of pine from the surrounding woods lingers in the air. A few more strokes and he's built enough momentum to reach the middle of the quarry. The canoe glides through the water until he angles his paddle to stop his forward motion. Small waves lap at the canoe, then all is still again.

He checks his watch, and he waits.

***

"Are you all right, Kevin? Do you need a glass of water?"

Kevin could barely make out Dr. Brier's words. His voice sounded muffled and far away, as if he were talking underwater. Ironic, considering the story Kevin was about to tell him.

"Sorry, guess I was gone for a second there, huh?" He rubbed his forehead. The skin of his face had grown sallow and loose. "Chemo brain. Been happening more often than I like to admit."

"But you're back with me now?"

"Yeah, I'm with you, Doc." Kevin searched his doctor's eyes. "But for how much longer?" He knew Dr. Brier wouldn't sugarcoat his answer. It's one of the reasons he liked him.

"Hard to say." Dr. Brier checked his notes. "We knew this last treatment was a long shot, so, barring some sort of miracle, best case is another six months, tops."

"And the worst?"

"Five to six weeks, if not less."

"Fewer."

"Excuse me?"

"For items you can count, like the number of weeks I have left to walk among the living, you use fewer, not less." He waved his hand. "Sorry, it's a habit of mine. A bad habit, if you ask my wife. She used to call me a grammar Nazi."

"Where is Kelli today?" Doctor Brier checked his notes again. "She's missed your last three appointments. It'd be good for both of you if she's here."

Kevin sighed. "No idea. If I'm being honest, she checked out a long time ago. Mentally, at least. I guess her body caught up with her head a few weeks back. I came home one day and there was a 'Dear John' letter on the table."

"I'm sorry to hear that. Are you okay?"

"Surprisingly, yeah. It's not how I would've handled it, but I don't blame her. Her letter said she felt our relationship had been going in circles for years, and she'd had enough. I guess dying put things in perspective for both of us."

"How so?"

Kevin ran his hand through what was left of his hair, the few strands the chemo and radiation hadn't stolen.

"Do you believe in fate? Predestination?"

"Are you trying to change the subject?"

"No, this actually ties into what we're talking about."

"That's a tough question. Do you want my medical opinion, or my honest opinion?"

"Whichever you're comfortable sharing."

"Medically, or rather, scientifically, there's no evidence for it. Things happen because they just do, not because they're supposed to." He paused.

"I sense a 'but' coming."

"But, as a doctor…" Dr. Brier stopped. He looked at Kevin's chart, then at the clock, then at the chart again. "That's weird," he said.

"What? Did you find something you missed?" Kevin tried to keep his voice even. He couldn't allow himself to hope. Not now.

"Sorry, no." Dr. Brier tapped the chart with his pen. "It's just, have we had this conversation before?"

"I don't think so, although now that you mention it, it does feel a little familiar. I've been having a lot of déjà vu lately too. Hope it's not contagious."

Dr. Brier laughed.

Kevin steered the conversation back on track. "You were saying…"

"Right. As a doctor, I've seen too many things happen I can't explain. Patients with a one percent chance of survival fully recover, while others with a ninety-nine percent chance never leave the hospital. Is that fate? Was the first patient destined to live, and the second destined to die? That's above my paygrade." He cocked his head. "Why do you ask? Do you think you were destined to get lung cancer, even though you're not a smoker…"

Kevin leaned back in his chair and considered his answer. "Honestly, yeah. Or something similar. I feel like I've been on this path my entire life," he said.

"We're all going to die at some point, so you could say that about everyone, couldn't you?"

"That's a fair point." He paused for a moment. "I wish I could explain it better. But for most of my life, I just had the sense that growing old wasn't in my future. So when I got the diagnosis, it just felt, I don't know if 'expected' is the right word, but it wasn't unexpected either, if that makes sense. Weird, huh?" He smiled. "It's a bit of a relief, if I'm being honest."

"I'm not sure I'm comfortable with where this is going." Dr. Brier leaned forward in his chair. "Should I be worried?"

Kevin shook his head. This was another reason he liked Dr. Brier. "I'm fine. Really, I am. I mean, don't get me wrong. This sucks. It sucks hard. And I sure as shit would change it if I could. But like I said, on some level, I knew something like this was going to happen. I've felt it since I was a kid. I don't think there's anything you could've done to change it either, so don't feel bad. We were bound, me and you, to end up right here, in this moment. That's why it feels so familiar, like déjà vu all over again. The treatments didn't work because they weren't supposed to work."

Dr. Brier picked up his prescription pad. "I can give you a prescription if you'd like. Something to take the edge off."

"Thanks, but I have enough prescriptions to last me a lifetime." He shrugged. "What's left of it, anyway." It was his turn to lean forward. "What I'd like is to tell you a story, if you'll let me."

Doctor Brier checked his watch, then his appointment book. "You're my last appointment, and it's my wife's turn to pick up our daughter, so sure, I have a little time. Let's hear it."

Kevin took a deep breath, then blew into his hands. Just thinking about that day brought on chills.

"Forty years ago this Thursday, I died. Drowned in Smith's Quarry, near Janas, Indiana, the town where I grew up. My friends did CPR and brought me back. Tommy said that right after I started breathing again, I was whispering about dead bodies at the bottom of the lake."

Dr. Brier's eyes widened. "Oh my god, that's horrible. You really died?"

"That's what they say."

"And the bodies? Were those real?"

"That's the sixty-four-thousand-dollar question, isn't it? Tommy swore that's what I said, but I don't remember it at all."

"Did you ever tell anyone?"

"And admit I drowned while we were swimming in the quarry?" He shook his head. "No way. Our parents would've tanned our hides."

He paused for a moment, deciding where to pick up again. "I don't know how much you know about limestone quarries, but southern Indiana is littered with them. A lot of the country's most famous buildings have limestone from the area: the National Cathedral, the Pentagon, even the Empire State Building."

"Did any of that come from your quarry?"

"I doubt it. Well, maybe the Pentagon. Did the Twin Towers have any limestone in them? The Alfred P. Murrah building? If so, I bet it was ours."

"You make it sound like the quarry was cursed."

"Not just the quarry. The entire area, including Janas, has seen more than its share of bad luck over the years. And it's not some cliched Indian curse either. Town legend says the Shawnee didn't even put up a fight when the settlers moved in. Just let 'em have it. Of course, no town wants to admit it's cursed, but even at the height of the limestone boom, Janas never prospered like the other towns did. So it was no surprise that Smith's Quarry was the first to go under when architects started replacing limestone with concrete and steel."

"That couldn't have been good for the town."

"That's an understatement. Put the whole place on life support. I don't know why my parents stayed. Who knows how differently my life would've turned out…" He dabbed at the corner of his eye. "Still, I had a pretty good run."

"It's not over yet."

"Your lips to God's ears." Kevin smiled. "There was an old workers' cabin near the quarry that was passed from one group of kids to another over the years," he said. "By the time me and my friends got it, I think the only thing holding the south wall together was band posters and centerfolds. Rest of the walls were covered with graffiti. The whole place smelled like teenage funk and dirty socks."

"That sounds—"

"Perfect? It was."

"Not the word I was going for, but you seem to have liked it."

"I loved it. Those summer days with my friends were the happiest of my life. We'd get buzzed on whatever alcohol we could steal from our parents' liquor cabinets and razz each other about the usual shit, mostly girls, sports, and puberty. Eventually, the talk would turn to the quarry, and how we were going to be the first to reach the bottom."

Dr. Brier tilted his head. "What do you mean?"

"Well, that's the thing about Smith's Quarry," Kevin said. "Nobody knows how deep it really is. Some quarries, the water's so blue you can see straight to the bottom, so you know what obstacles are in the way when you dive, like old machinery or slag piles. But not Smith's Quarry. That water was dark. Scary dark. Even walking a few yards out from the shore, you were lucky if you could see past your knees."

Dr. Brier jotted down a few notes. "Was the water polluted? Did the quarry use any toxic chemicals? It'd be interesting to see if other townspeople have had cancers like yours."

"Probably. Although I doubt they ever tested it. Certainly wouldn't admit it if they did. Water never smelled bad though. Of course, no one knows exactly where the water comes from. Has to be an underground spring somewhere down there. That's why it's always so cold, you know. The first couple feet near the surface, where the sun can penetrate, isn't bad. But once you get deeper than that, the water temperature can drop ten, twenty degrees faster than a heartbeat."

Dr. Brier tapped his forehead. "I vaguely remember reading an article about a rash of drownings we had one summer in a quarry near here," he said. "If I recall correctly, the reporter said more often than not it's the cold water that kills you, that the kids went into shock before they knew what hit them. Is that what happened to you?"

"Not quite." Kevin coughed into his hand. Flecks of blood dotted his palm. Dr. Brier handed him a tissue. "Thanks. Do you think I could get some water too?"

"Sure." Doctor Brier grabbed two bottles from his office mini fridge. He handed one to Kevin and sat back down. "I'm sorry for all the interruptions." He opened his bottle and took a sip. "I'm just looking for any clues that may point us to another line of treatment."

Kevin took a long drink before answering. "I know you mean well, Doc, but you're not gonna find a cure in this story. You're just chasing your own tail at this point. Maybe I should stop."

"No, please, keep going. I think it's important to you, and I'd like to hear how it ends."

"Okay, thanks." He took another drink, then resumed his tale.

"The old timers in town loved to tell stories about the place. Like how the government sent a team down to find the spring that fed it, except they all disappeared, and the Feds spread a bunch of hush money around to cover it up. Or how Big Jim, whose grandfather retired and gave Jim Sr. the gas station right about the same time that hush money was being handed out, swore he caught the same fish five times one summer. Same markings, same hook scars, same everything. Said it tasted just as delicious every time too." He chuckled at the memory. "Billy's Uncle Frank once told me it was haunted by the ghost of some kids who'd swam too deep trying to reach the bottom. Pretty sure he was just trying to scare us."

"You didn't believe him?"

"About the kids? No. Story like that we'd have heard about from more than just Billy's uncle. But the rest seemed plausible. We knew there'd been plenty of workers who'd drowned out there over the years. Most times they'd recover the bodies."

"Most times?"

"Like I said, nobody knew how deep Smith's Quarry was. Lots of people, kids and adults, tried to reach the bottom over the years, but nobody ever did. I probably got closer than anybody the day I died.

"I'd been training all summer, holding my breath and swimming a little deeper each day. By the time August rolled around, I could hold my breath for nearly three minutes on a good day. If anyone was going to reach the bottom, it was me. I'd borrowed a pair of swim goggles from my cousin, and we duct taped a flashlight inside a plastic bag. We had about a hundred and fifty feet of rope from shorter pieces we tied together. It didn't look safe, but I trusted Billy's knots. Don't know why. Billy'd never been in the scouts or anything. I just knew they'd hold.

"Our plan was pretty simple. I'd swim down as fast as I could. At sixty seconds, they'd give the rope a tug to let me know how much time I had left. After another fifteen to twenty seconds, if I hadn't turned around, they'd start pulling me back up. I strapped a knife to my leg in case the rope got caught on anything.

"There was no wind that day, so the water was perfectly still. We paddled the canoe out to the middle of the quarry. I checked the knots one last time, turned the flashlight on, and jumped in.

"A few feet down, the water turned dark. A few feet after that, the temperature dropped. The cold slammed my nuts up into my throat, but I was ready for it. I swam as hard as I could until I felt the first tug. I still had more air in my lungs, so I kept swimming downward. Then a funny thing happened: the water cleared up. I mean, it was still darker than a coal miner's asshole, pardon my French, but the light from the flashlight was going farther than before. And there, at the edge of the light, I could make out the shape of...*something*. It had to be the bottom. Or something *on* the bottom. I was so close, it was literally within reach. I just needed to swim down a little farther...

"And then everything went to shit. They must have been worried about me up top, because they jerked that rope something awful. The tug caught me by surprise, and I dropped the flashlight. Even worse, I lost my air and panicked. My arms got tangled in the rope. My lungs were on fire and stars exploded in my eyes and then...nothing.

"The next thing I remember, Tommy's blowing in my mouth and Billy's pounding on my chest and I'm coughing up buckets of dark water. Tommy said I wasn't breathing when they pulled me into the canoe and they'd been doing CPR for at least three minutes and they had no idea what they were going to tell my mom and then suddenly I was back. It wasn't until later that night, just before we went to sleep, that Tommy told me what else had happened. He said right after I coughed up that first lungful of water, I started whispering awful things about dead bodies at the bottom of the quarry. Even worse, it wasn't my voice. Said I sounded like someone a lot older. He figured it had to be from coughing up all that water, right? I didn't remember anything after that rope tug though, so I don't know if he was playing with me or not."

Kevin finished his water and leaned back in his chair. "So, whaddaya think?"

"I think that's quite the story," Doctor Brier said. "Is that why you weren't surprised by the cancer? All the water you swallowed? Or is it a bit more existential? That you couldn't cheat death forever?"

Before Kevin could answer, Dr. Brier's receptionist rang in. His wife was on the line and said it was urgent. "I'm sorry, Kevin, I have to take this. Can you have a seat in the waiting room and we'll make an appointment once I'm off the phone?"

"Sure, Doc. Thanks for listening." Kevin walked out of the office, waved to the receptionist, and left the building for the last time.

***

Kevin can't hold his breath nearly as long as he used to, but he's not worried. There's no need to save enough air for a return trip to the surface; this time it's a one-way ticket straight to the bottom. He's stuffed his pockets full of rocks and tied a heavy chain around his waist. It should help him sink faster.

It also guarantees he can't chicken out and change his mind.

If he's lucky, he'll finally learn if Tommy was telling the truth about the day he died. If not, maybe it'll be *his* ghost the old timers warn the kids about. Either way, it's better than sitting around waiting for the cancer to take him.

He double checks the chain again. It only weighs about twenty pounds, but carrying it the fifty yards from the parking lot to the canoe wiped him out. The last thing he needs is for it to slip off, so he's fastened it with zip ties to his belt loops to make sure it doesn't.

Next, he puts on his dive mask and clips a mini scuba light to the strap. That should give him a couple feet of illumination. Finally, he picks up a high-powered diving light. It's bigger and brighter than the flashlight he used as a kid. With his free hand, he puts a plastic baggie over his hand and the light, then duct tapes the baggie shut around his wrist. He's not going to drop it this time. If anyone ever finds his body, it'll give the old timers something to talk about.

When the sun finally breaks over the horizon, Kevin is ready. Morning birds greet the day with songs from the surrounding trees. The water is like glass. He swings his feet over the edge of the canoe and basks in the warmth of the rising sun.

He takes one long, final breath.

Holds it.

And slides below the surface.

The water is darker and colder than he remembers. He turns on his headlight and swims downward. It takes a few strokes to figure out how to make the extra weight around his waist work in his favor, but once he's sussed out the balance, he goes down even faster than he'd hoped. His headlamp barely penetrates the darkness, but it helps. He'll turn on the bigger light when he gets closer to the bottom.

He continues to force himself downward, expelling some air out of his lungs to buy himself a little more time. It feels like he's been swimming forever, but he knows it couldn't be more than a minute or so. His lungs are burning, and stars dot his peripheral vision.

The water begins to clear right before he crashes into the bottom. He struggles to orient himself as unconsciousness threatens to pull him under. He turns on the dive flashlight and shines it around. Dozens of bodies lie scattered about the quarry floor. Some are wearing scuba goggles with dead headlamps. Some have flashlights and a plastic bag taped to their wrist. All have chains around their waist.

He screams, expelling the last bit of oxygen from his lungs. Cold, dark water rushes in to take its place. As the horror of his situation sinks in, the memories of what he saw all those years ago come flooding back. How many times has he made this dive? How many times has he traveled this cursed loop, to die here at the bottom only to resurface decades earlier, to that very moment when his friends revived him? How many more times *would* he travel it? He knows he'll succumb yet again, helpless against the pull, the endless cycle of life and death. He focuses his dying energy around one final thought, a lifeline thrown backward through time.

Please remember.

Remember.

Re…

***

"Holy crap, you're alive!" Tommy yells when Kevin finally opens his eyes and coughs up the first lungful of dark water. He and Billy have been doing CPR for a few minutes now, and are ready to give up when Kevin opens his eyes. In between coughs, he whispers something.

Tommy leans in and tries to decipher what his best friend is saying. "…bodies, so many bodies, *my* bodies, so many…"

CAN YOU DIG IT?

"Bet you can't guess what it is," Mike said as he handed his wife her birthday gift.

"Well, it looks like you just gift-wrapped a shovel, but that's a little too obvious…" Lisa turned it over and inspected the bow. "Still, if it looks like a shovel and it feels like a shovel, I'm guessing it's a spa day, or maybe a mani-pedi…?"

"Nope, it's a shovel! I knew you'd never figure it out."

"You got me." She rolled her eyes as she unwrapped her gift.

"I found it at an estate sale out off County Line Road," he said, ignoring her sarcasm. "Guy had all kinds of garden tools and equipment. The woman running the sale told me he used to be a gravedigger at Oak Lawn."

"Wait, you don't think he used this to…"

"I doubt it. Unless he was getting 'buried' at work."

She winced.

"I mean, there's bringing your work home, and then there's *really* bringing your work home. I'm sure he just used this one for gardening."

"I hope so. Otherwise, it's a pretty morbid gift."

Mike shook his head. "As morbid as some shovel made by child labor in China? This one has history. The handle's already broken in, the blade's good and sharp. If it could talk, I bet it'd have some great 'veggie-tales.'"

Lisa groaned. "It sounds like she's made quite the impression on you."

"What makes you think it's a she? Shovels are obviously male. You push it into the moist earth, then pull it out, then push it back in, over and over and over…"

"Wow. This just got really weird."

"Sorry. It's better than last year's gift though, right?"

"We agreed to never talk about that again. I still can't believe you thought I'd wear that."

"Yeah, yeah." He waved her off, then pointed to the shovel. "So, do you like it?"

She ran her hands over the nicks and scratches on the handle, then picked at a flake of rust on the blade. "I love it," she said.

***

That night he dreamt of open graves.

***

They'd both worked from home since the start of the pandemic. Mike was an accountant; she led a team of ten salespeople scattered across four time zones. Her company was coming up on the end of a big push, so she'd been working even more evening and weekend hours than normal, leaving little time for gardening. She'd had to cut her daily runs to every other day, and then every few days, and then once or twice a week, if she was lucky. Since her birthday, though, she'd starting running every evening again, which made Mike happy for her. Of course, she still found time to put together an extensive "Honey-Do" list between conference calls and Zoom meetings. That meant lots of trips to the nursery, and lots of holes to dig. So many holes. He was getting way more use out of her gift than she had up to this point.

He wasn't complaining though. In fact, he was having a blast. He knew it sounded silly, but digging holes with that shovel felt *right*. Like it's what he was meant to do. He'd even dug a few that weren't on her list, just for fun. Even now, sitting at his desk going over some stupid spreadsheets, his mind was on digging. The solid *thrum* in his forearms as the blade penetrated the earth. The endless possibilities of that first shovelful of dirt and clay. The feeling of accomplishment when the hole was dug.

Now, when he looked at places in the yard or the woods behind their house, he thought of how big a hole he could dig. How deep he could make it.

At night, he dreamt about what he could put in it.

***

"Have you seen the Fahertys' cat?" Lisa asked over their usual Saturday breakfast of blueberry pancakes. "Marsha said they haven't seen him for a couple days."

"No, but I'll keep an eye out for him." He gathered up their dishes. "Since you're working all day again, I'm gonna take a hike out back."

After he loaded the dishwasher, they walked out onto the back porch together. "You haven't seen the shovel, have you?" he asked.

She laughed. "Why in the world do you need that?"

"You never know when you might find some buried treasure," he said.

"Or need to bury something," a voice in his head whispered.

"I think I saw it by the back fence."

"Whadaya know, there it is." The shovel was leaning against the fence by the back gate. "Weird, I don't remember leaving it there. I swear that thing has a mind of its own sometimes." He grabbed the shovel, waved goodbye to Lisa, and headed into the woods.

It was a beautiful spring morning, and the birds were practically singing "Zip-A-Dee-Do-Dah." About twenty minutes from the house, a sickly sweet stench of something recently dead interrupted his reverie. Maybe it was a good thing he'd brought the shovel after all.

A fox peeked its head around a tree to his left. He'd seen it around the neighborhood before, darting between houses when it thought no one was looking. He'd even tossed a few scraps meant for the compost bin over the back fence for it last week. Today, he'd been dropping the occasional almond from his bag of trail mix. He hated almonds. As much as Lisa loved almond milk, he just couldn't bring himself to drink the stuff. Milk was supposed to come from mammals. Squeeze a teat, get some milk. Almonds had no teats.

Laughing to himself at the image of a giant almond with a large, pendulous udder hanging from its underside, he almost tripped over a fresh mound of dirt. Glancing around, he noticed several more. He thought they were too big for an animal to have made them. In fact, they looked like someone had dug a hole and filled it back up, like that scene in *Cool Hand Luke.* "What's that dirt doing in my hole?" he asked the fox. As odd as it was, though, since he and Lisa didn't own the land behind their house, there was nothing he could do. He made a mental note to ask Lisa about it when he got home.

Mike took a break under an old oak. The sun was warm on his face, and he had trouble keeping his eyes open. It wasn't long before he dozed off.

When he awoke, the sun was far lower than it should have been. He checked his phone. He'd been asleep for hours. Lisa must be buried in sales forecasts for her not to have sent a text checking up on him.

He moved to rub the sleep out of his eyes and froze. His hands were filthy, and he had a large blood blister on his left palm. He looked around, trying to get his bearings. Someone had stuck the shovel blade-down in a pile of dirt about ten feet away.

Despite the day's warmth, cold sweat ran down his spine.

He walked over and grabbed the shovel. On the other side of the mound was a small hole. *"Grave,"* the voice in his head whispered. The fox lay crumpled at the bottom, its skull crushed. Blood had pooled and soaked into the dirt. Flies buzzed around its head.

He gagged, then turned and threw up. He wiped strings of vomit from his mouth. Had someone snuck up here while he was sleeping? Who would do something like this? He ignored the tiny voice asking about the dirt on his hands.

He couldn't leave the fox in this condition. "Sorry, buddy," he said. A cloud of flies flew up in protest when the first shovel of dirt hit the fox's head.

***

Mike went straight to the bathroom when he got home. "Gonna take a shower," he yelled. Lisa grunted affirmation from her office down the hall. "Need to throw my clothes in the wash too. Got some serious stink on them."

He peeled off his clothes as the shower heated up, then wiped steam off the mirror. His face was streaked with red.

That had to be clay, right?

In the shower, he scrubbed himself raw and watched the crimson water swirl down the drain. He stayed there until the hot water ran out.

He towel-dried his hair, then took his dirty clothes to the laundry room. He was surprised to see Lisa's running clothes in the washer. She must really be distracted to throw them in and forget to turn the machine on. He threw his in on top, added the soap, and started the wash. As he went to leave, he noticed her sneakers tossed in the corner, their bottoms caked in mud. Had she gone for a run while he slept under the tree? Had she seen someone kill the fox? Had she seen *him* kill the fox? He went upstairs to ask her, but she'd shut her office door and stuck a "Do Not Disturb" sticky above the handle. Figuring he'd ask her later, he went to the kitchen to start dinner.

By the time she joined him, he'd decided not to bring it up. He wanted to forget about that poor fox.

That night, he dreamt he was digging in an open field. But he was in someone else's body. Someone who *worked* for a living. His hands were calloused and rough, fingers gnarled and bent like an old tree branch. His thick forearms were marked with scars and ropy with muscle. Skin like old leather, weathered from years spent working in the elements. He'd spent his career behind a desk. The hardest work he'd ever done was digging holes for Lisa. And honestly, he didn't consider that to be work. Not anymore. When he held that shovel, when he moved the earth, he felt fulfilled.

He lifted a shovelful of dirt from the pile and tossed it into the grave.

Lisa's eyes opened when the dirt hit her face.

Mike jerked awake, his underwear sticky with semen.

***

On his walk the next evening, he noticed several flyers for missing pets. His mind went to the mounds of dirt he'd seen behind their house, but he buried that thought fast.

The house was empty when he got home. The light in Lisa's office was on and her car was still in the garage. She'd probably gone out for a run.

He poured a glass of wine and stood over the sink, looking out into the back yard. There was a light moving through the woods behind their house. He watched it for another minute or two. There was definitely someone out there.

He threw on his jacket, grabbed a flashlight, and headed out the backdoor. His footsteps crunched along the gravel path. The woods were strangely silent.

By the time he stepped through the back gate, the light had stopped moving.

He picked up his pace once he hit the trail.

"Hello? Is anyone out there? Lisa, is that you?"

He swept the woods with his flashlight as he walked. No sign of anyone. He was alone. For the moment, at least.

It took a few minutes to reach the light. It was their camping lantern. Someone had left it sitting atop a pile of loose dirt.

"Lisa, are you out here?"

Silence.

He pulled out his phone and called her. Almost immediately, her phone rang from nearby.

"Lisa? Come on, this isn't funny." He picked up the lantern. On the other side of the dirt pile was Lisa's shovel. Next to that, hidden from the trail, was an enormous hole.

"An enormous grave," the voice whispered.

He held the lantern out and looked around. Lisa's phone lay near the edge of the hole. It continued to ring. He bent down to pick it up when Lisa stepped out from behind the tree.

"Honey, what's going on?" he asked. His knees cracked when he stood up. "What are you doing out here?"

She didn't answer.

"Did you dig this hole?"

She picked up the shovel. "It's not a hole," she said. "Not anymore."

She swung the shovel so fast he didn't have time to react. The *crack* of his skull fracturing echoed like a gunshot. He fell backward. His neck snapped when he hit the bottom of the hole, and his limbs went numb.

Lisa looked down at him. "It's a grave."

Mike lay there, unable to move, as she threw the first shovelful of dirt over his face.

"And every grave needs a body."

Sharing is Caring

Tommy shoved the smaller boy in the chest. "You're gonna give me all your candy," he said. "Or else."

Sammy looked up at the older boy. "Or else what?"

"Do you really want to find out?"

"No." Sammy's shoulders sagged, and he held out his candy bucket. Tommy grabbed it, poured it all into his large sack, even the Raisinets, then tossed the empty bucket back. It bounced off Sammy's stomach and landed on the ground.

Tommy puffed out his chest, towering over the smaller boy. "If you tell anyone, I'll do worse than steal your candy, got it?" He shoved Sammy backward again. "Now get out of here!"

Tommy laughed as Sammy's retreating figure disappeared into the darkness. "Thanks for the candy, stupid!"

Counting Sammy, Tommy had stolen candy from four kids so far. And there was still one more stop on his list. This would be his best Halloween haul ever.

He tossed the sack over his shoulder and started walking. At a house near the intersection of Maple and Elm, he stepped behind a row of hedges and waited for Mikey to come home. The little squirt was new to the neighborhood, and Tommy hadn't had a chance to show him who ran things around here. Tonight was the perfect opportunity to fix that while upping his candy count.

Official trick or treating hours were nearly over, so he figured Mikey would be along sooner rather than later. While he waited, he ate. By the time he heard Mikey coming down the street, his feet were buried beneath a pile of empty wrappers.

It surprised him to see Rose and Annie walking alongside Mikey. *Little guy's got game,* he thought. Tommy almost felt bad about embarrassing him in front of his girlfriends.

Almost.

Tommy stepped out in front of the three children. "You have something of mine," he said, pointing his finger at Mikey.

Mikey's eyes widened. "What are you taking about?"

"You have my candy." Tommy reached for Mikey's bucket.

Rose slapped at Tommy's hand. "Leave him alone, Tommy. It's our candy, not yours."

Annie stepped next to Rose. "Yeah, it's ours. We put all of it in one bucket to share. And you can't have any."

"That true, Mikey?" Tommy stared down at the smaller boy. "You're not gonna share with me?"

Mikey looked at the two girls. "Maybe we can give him a couple pieces?"

"Don't do it, Mikey," Annie said.

"Please? It's ours," Rose said.

Mikey looked at the candy, then back at Rose and Annie. Tommy pushed the two girls aside and grabbed the bucket.

"Hey!" Mikey yelled. "I said maybe a couple pieces!"

"Whatever." Tommy shoved Mikey to the ground. He landed on his butt and sat there, upper lip trembling.

"Aw, is the baby gonna cry?" Tommy dumped their candy into his sack, dropped the empty bucket onto Mikey's lap, and walked away.

Ten minutes later, he was relaxing in the clubhouse he'd built in the woods with his friends last summer. He turned on the lantern, grabbed a stack of comics, sat down, and unwrapped a piece of candy. He lost track of time as he ate. A knock on the door brought him back. He was sitting on the floor, surrounded by candy wrappers, an unopened comic in his lap. He looked in the sack. It was empty. *Shit!* He hadn't saved any candy for his friends. He gathered up the wrappers and stuffed them back in the sack, then threw it onto a pile of rags in the corner.

"About time you guys showed up," he said as he opened the door.

His friends weren't there. Instead, Mikey looked up at him. He was holding his bucket out.

"I want my candy back," Mikey said.

"Sorry, you can't have it. Now scram." Tommy stepped back into the clubhouse and swung the door shut. Mikey stuck his foot in the doorway and stopped it from closing.

"I said I want my candy back."

"And I said you can't have it. Now get outta here before I do something you're gonna regret."

"We want our candy back too," said Sammy. Franky stood next to him.

"Well, this is getting interesting," Tommy said, cracking his knuckles. "Three against one, huh?"

"Try five," Jason said as he and Chucky joined the other boys.

Rose and Annie came walking down the path. "Make that seven."

"Wait a minute, I never took your candy." Tommy pointed at Jason and Chucky. "Or did I? Y'all look alike in your little baby costumes."

"Give us our candy, Tommy," Rose and Annie said.

"Careful." Tommy's eyes narrowed. "Don't think I won't hit a girl."

"Candy," Franky grunted. "Now."

Tommy gave an exaggerated sigh. "Fine, I'll get it. There's more than enough to share. Just hold on a second, okay?" He looked down at Mikey's foot. "Do you mind?" Mikey moved his foot back so Tommy could shut the door.

A minute later, he came back outside and walked to the fire pit, dragging the candy sack behind him. He made a show of how heavy it was.

"You babies really outdid yourselves this year. Here you go." He emptied the sack onto the ground. Over a hundred empty wrappers tumbled out, forming a pile in the ashes. The children shared a look of disappointment, then indignation.

"You should see your faces!" Tommy sneered. "Like I was really gonna share any of it. I already ate it all, you idiots!"

"We figured as much," Mikey said. Moonlight caught the edge of the butcher's knife in his hand.

"Figured," Franky echoed, picking up a large piece of wood.

Chucky pulled out a kitchen knife, Sammy a broken bottle. Rose had a loop of clothesline. Jason held up a small machete, while Annie revealed a croquet mallet she'd been hiding behind her back.

Too late, Tommy realized he was in trouble. "You guys better get out of here," he said, raising his voice as he took a step back toward the clubhouse. "My buddies will be here any second now." He swung his head around, hoping his friends could hear him. Chucky stuck his foot out. Tommy tripped over it and fell on his rear.

"Hold him still," Annie yelled. "I'll make sure he can't run away!"

The other children dropped their weapons and jumped on Tommy, punching and kicking him. He was big for his age, but there were too many of them. It was over before it even began. They dragged him into the woods behind the cabin, then tied each hand and foot to a different tree before going back for their weapons.

They formed a loose circle around Tommy's outstretched body. Annie swung her mallet and shattered his right ankle. When he screamed,

Sammy shoved a piece of dirty burlap into his mouth, and Franky smashed his head with the log. Tommy's body went limp.

The children fell on him then, a pack of feral animals. Blades flashed and blood sprayed as they slit Tommy open from neck to navel.

Tommy's stomach was full of half-digested candy, much of it still recognizable.

"Who had a Zagnut?" Mikey asked, extracting a glob of chocolate from Tommy's abdomen.

"Me," Franky grunted.

"Here you go then." Mikey handed the wet lump to Franky, who ate it without looking.

"Chocolate good," he said.

Next, Mikey pulled out a dripping mass of peanuts and nougat. "Looks like what's left of a Payday," he said. "Any takers?"

Sammy nodded. Mikey handed it to him.

Mikey dug around some more in Tommy's guts. He used his knife to slice open a coil of intestine. "Looks like Red Vines," he said, holding up a couple small chunks of red licorice.

"Gross!" said Rose. "Twizzlers are so much better!"

Jason severed the end of Tommy's bowels from his rectum, squeezing the intestine as he unspooled it. Rose licked her lips as a long turd packed with bits of Raisinets, M&M's, and Hershey's Kisses slid out, steaming in the dirt.

"Still a lot left to choose from," Chucky said, poking in Tommy's guts with the tip of his knife. "Let's dig in!"

One by one, they buried their faces in Tommy's stomach and ate their share.

THE OUTPOST, OUTSIDE

Cory had just finished updating the entry logs when the alarm sounded. Movement in Quadrant Three. The ground sensors hadn't been tripped, but something in the area must have startled the bird. He rewound the footage again and watched for any signs of the infected.

Jerry rolled his chair over to Cory's desk. "What do you think it is?"

Cory shrugged. "Probably nothing."

"I hope so," Jerry said. His voice trembled a bit at the edges. "Ain't no way I'm going out there."

"Don't worry about it. I'm sure everything's fine."

"You don't have to tell me twice." He got up and headed for the door. "I'm going to the cafeteria. You want anything?"

"Nah, I'm good."

"Suit yourself, man. Your brother's making Cheez Whiz casserole."

"No thanks. I ate enough of that stuff growing up." Cory turned back to the monitor. Once he heard the door shut behind him, he breathed a sigh of relief. The last person he wanted to take outside was Jerry. If you wanted to know the similarities between string theory and string cheese, Jerry was your man. But if you wanted someone you could count on when the crap hit the fan, Cory would sooner trust his back to HAL 9000.

Cory rewound the footage and watched it again. He zoomed in. There, in the upper left corner of the screen, he thought *maybe* he saw something in the trees move right before the bird took off, but the footage was too blurry to be sure.

He leaned back in his chair. Maybe the bird was just hungry. Or horny. Do birds even get horny? He knew they laid eggs, but that's where his knowledge of avian reproductive practices ended. He couldn't remember any of his friends ever bragging about doing it "birdie-style," but that didn't mean birds never let their freak feathers fly. Too bad Doug hadn't recruited an ornithologist for this mission. Or even brought a bird book, for that matter. He made a mental note to request a data search on the subject. It might take a couple days, as net access was spotty this far out. And when it was up, everyone wanted on. *That's what she said!* He snorted at his own lame joke and then watched the footage again.

***

Although they were only born three years apart, Cory had never been close with his little brother. So he was shocked when Doug asked him to join the mission.

"We could really use someone like you this time out," Doug said.

"Someone like me?" Cory cracked his knuckles. "Aren't you worried about getting your butt kicked in front of your team?"

"Not as worried as I am about them getting their butts kicked."

"By who?"

"That's classified. I just need you to protect them."

"From what?"

"That's classified too."

"Then I'm gonna have to say no." Cory pushed his chair back from the table.

"Cory, wait." Doug looked around the room. "Look, I can't go into all the details right now, but there's been an outbreak in Sector Five. Roughly half the population is infected."

"Infected with what?"

Doug didn't answer.

"Let me guess. That's classified too, right?" Cory ran his hand through his hair. "Fifty percent? That seems pretty high. Are you sure about those numbers?"

"Plus or minus two percent, but yeah, we're sure." Doug paused. "I've probably said too much already, but you *are* my brother, so I'm gonna bend the rules a little bit more."

"Gee, thanks."

"Reports from the field indicate the infected seem to share some sort of hive mind. They seek each other out and travel in groups, spreading the infection as they go. It's up to us to find a cure, or at least contain the outbreak."

"Sounds like you need more bug hunters," Cory said. "Not someone like me."

"You're right. I don't need someone *like* you," Doug said. "I need you." He slid a file across the table. "These are the guys I've recruited so far. They're experts in their fields, but do you really think any of them can handle themselves outside a lab?"

Cory flipped through the file. He didn't recognize any of the names, but he could tell by their headshots his brother was right; it looked like half of them hadn't even hit puberty yet. Plus or minus two percent.

He knew Doug would never admit it, but something about this mission had him spooked. It's the only reason he would ask for help.

Cory closed the folder and slid it back. "What's in it for me?"

Doug smiled. "Besides the joy of us hanging out together for a few weeks?"

"Yeah, besides that."

"How about the chance to protect some of the brightest minds of our generation?"

"Not good enough."

"How about we really need you on this one, Cory? *I* really need you." A flush crept up Doug's cheeks. "Would it help if I said please?"

Cory mulled it over. His gut said to walk away, but he knew their mom would expect him to take care of his little brother. Life would be so much easier if he were an only child.

"Okay," he finally said, "I'm in."

It only took a couple days for Cory to second-guess his decision. He could handle his brother, but the other guys were way too Poindexter for his liking: plenty of book-smarts, but the social graces of a herd of flatulent goats. If they weren't fighting over who dealt it, they were arguing over who smelt it.

Baby brother was definitely going to pay for this if they made it back.

***

Cory debated whether to tell his brother about the bird, but decided against it. Base security was his responsibility. Anything out of the ordinary, he had to check it out. In person. You don't trust a mission like this to a monitor. Other outposts had made that mistake in the past; his wouldn't.

Besides, Doug would want to tell the others, and then they'd spend the next three hours arguing about whether the infected were nearby and what to do if the outpost was overrun and whether the Flash could outrun Quicksilver and whether the element quicksilver was poisonously beautiful or beautifully poisonous and, in the end, they'd agree to send Cory out to investigate, but by then it'd be too late.

He took a last look at the footage, checked the coordinates, and stepped outside. The pneumatic door, designed to shut silently, still sounded too loud to his ears out here under the overcast grey sky. He scanned the vines and deadfall at the edge of the woods and waited.

Nothing moved.

Without taking his eyes off the woods, he reached into his pack, pulled out the micro-sprayer, and coated himself in a protective mist. The boys in the lab thought this new aerosol would give him about thirty minutes of protection from the contagion, but they had no way to know for sure until it was tested in the field. Which technically made him a guard *and* a guinea pig.

He was getting too old for this crap. Still, *something* had spooked that bird. And he was pretty sure it wasn't a birdie booty call.

He knew opening the outside door had triggered an alarm back in the control room, so the lab monkeys were probably watching him on the monitor by now. He also knew none of them were brave enough to join him, so he was surprised when the door opened and Doug walked out. Maybe little brother was finally growing a pair after all.

"You actually gonna join me?"

"Out there?" Doug stole a quick glance at the woods, then turned his attention back to Cory. "No way. I just came out to get the sprayer back. We can't take a chance on you losing it."

Cory spat. "Should've known you couldn't hang." He handed the bottle to Doug.

Doug tucked it into his pack and gave Cory a vidcam. "I need you to wear this. It'll stream everything back to the lab in real time, so we can see what you see. It streams audio too, so watch your language."

Cory held the vidcam at arm's length and stuck his middle finger up toward the lens.

"Really? You better hope Mom doesn't see that."

"You better make sure she doesn't," Cory said. "Or this contagion will be the least of your worries."

Doug handed him an earpiece. "I need you to wear this too. If we see anything we want you to check out, I'll let you know."

Doug went back inside. Cory was on his own. He put the earpiece in and gave the vidcam a final one-finger salute before clipping it on his hat.

Part of him wished his brother were a little braver, but the more rational part was glad Doug hadn't wanted to tag along. Going out by himself like this was dangerous enough, but taking his brother would only make it worse. He could move faster on his own, and he wouldn't have to worry about being a babysitter.

He was just a few yards into the woods when his earpiece crackled to life. *"Hey, Cory, you doing okay?"* Speak of the devil. His brother's disembodied voice sounded even younger in his ear.

"I'm fine, numbnuts. How's life back in the nursery? Mom come by to tuck you babies in yet?"

"Very funny. She did call earlier, though. Wants us to come home for dinner sometime."

"Finally, some real food." Cory's eyes narrowed. "Now shut your face hole. Time to show you boys how it's done."

Cory followed the trail deeper into the woods. He was only a few hundred yards away from the outpost now, but already it felt like a different world. The wind had picked up. Branches swayed overhead, swallowing the light. Shadows pulsed and danced along the edge of the trail, playing havoc with his depth perception.

He stopped.

"I'm losing the light out here. You knuckleheads see anything?" He tried to keep his tone light. Couldn't let the lab coats know the shadows were getting to him.

"Vid feed's pretty dark, but we're also tracking you on GPS. It looks like the path forks up ahead. Go left."

"Roger that." Cory continued forward, slowly, his eyes constantly checking for movement, his ears cocked for any sound that would indicate the presence of the infected: an errant twig snap; rustling underbrush; or, worst of all, the high-pitched, maniacal giggling that signaled an oncoming horde.

He reached the fork. The path to the right headed up, toward daylight. The path on the left tracked down and disappeared into darkness about twenty yards from his position.

"You sure you want me to go left?"

"Did I stutter? Wait, you're not scared, are you?" He could hear the grin in Doug's voice. *"Do I need to send Jerry out to rescue you?"*

"That's pretty brave talk coming from someone who still sleeps with a nightlight." Cory gritted his teeth. "I won't forget this."

"Sorry, man, just busting your balls. Be careful out there, okay? Don't make me tell Mom I lost you."

"You won't get rid of me that easy."

Somewhere in the darkness, a twig snapped.

Cory stopped in his tracks. "Did you hear that?"

Someone was down there. Maybe a *bunch* of someones. And they clearly weren't concerned with stealth.

"Hold on, we're running a scan."

Cory wiped cold sweat from the back of his neck while he waited. Did Doug sound worried?

A single, manic giggle floated up from the darkness. Then another, and another, and another, each building on the last, until the laughter echoed throughout the woods just below him.

"Talk to me, Doug!" Cory shook while his mind fought against his body's flight response. His mind was losing. "What's going on?"

The infected were getting closer.

"Cory, they're coming!" Doug's voice screamed in his ear. *"Get out of there! Now!"*

He ran, all the time looking for somewhere to hide. No place felt safe.

The laughter was all around him now. Had they circled around behind him on his way in? If so, Doug's team had severely underestimated any effect the infection had on intelligence. Could the hive mind actually make them smarter?

Cory was near panic. The trail hadn't been this long and narrow coming in, had it? The light was almost gone, and he tripped over rocks and roots every few feet. A branch hit his face, raked his eyes, and knocked his hat off. *Shit!* He'd lost the vidcam. Doug couldn't help him now; he was on his own. He ran off the path and crouched behind a tree. He needed to get his bearings, but things were moving too fast to process. The infected could be anywhere—hiding behind that outcropping of rocks, lurking in those bushes to the left, coiled on a branch right above him!—just waiting to strike.

Waiting for a chance to spread their disease.

To infect him with their cooties.

Cory swore this was the last time he'd ever go camping in a Boys-Only fort built by nerds.

THE SANTADVENT KILLER

"Drop the knife, Jack. It's over."

"No way." Jack pressed the edge of the blade against Santa's throat, drawing a bead of blood. "Not when I'm so close."

"I'm not letting you kill him," I said, the gun steady in my hand. "Not like the others."

The "others" in question were the 13 mall Santas Jack had tortured and killed over the past 13 days. One fresh kill per day, each more creative than the last. The news media had dubbed him the "Santadvent Killer." The first victim he'd merely decapitated with an axe. Left a giant snowball where his head should be, complete with corncob pipe, button nose, and eyes made out of coal. The 13th, yesterday's victim, had candy canes shoved into his eye sockets. The eyes were sitting next to a glass of milk by the fireplace. He'd impaled the poor guy on top of a Christmas tree; shoved it straight up his ass like he was a tree topper. He'd tied his hands to the ceiling to hold the body in place, using razor wire wrapped in silver and green tinsel. The branches dripped shit and blood.

"Put the knife down slowly." I gestured with my gun. "You're not gonna make it through the entire calendar. This advent countdown stops now."

"Can we talk about that name?" Jack scowled. "What a lame portmanteau. It's like they're not even trying."

I didn't know what a portmanteau was, but he didn't need to know that.

"Do you have a better name?" I was stalling, trying to buy time until my backup arrived. "Let Santa go and maybe we can get the press to use it instead."

"If they're just going to shove two words together, off the top of my head I'd suggest 'North Poleaxe.'" He chuckled. "Or what about 'Santa Claws'?" He curled his free hand into a claw and swiped at Santa's face.

"Wouldn't work," Santa mumbled.

He was still alive, thank God. Jack had zip tied him to a chair next to a Christmas tree. His face looked like raw hamburger. Candy canes peeked out from several incisions across his torso, and Jack had chopped the toes off his right foot. A puddle of dark blood congealed on the floor. An axe lay nearby. Jack had cauterized the wound with a few lumps of burning coal. They were still glowing.

Jack pressed the knife deeper into Santa's neck, drawing a fresh line of blood. "Why wouldn't it work?" he asked.

Santa spat out a wad of bloody phlegm. A tooth bounced across the concrete floor. "It's a visual pun," he said. "You need to see it spelled out for people to get it. Otherwise, it still sounds like Santa Claus."

"Whatever." Jack clubbed him on the back of the head.

"Why'd you do it?" I asked.

"I needed to get his attention."

"Whose?"

"Santa's, of course."

My jaw dropped. "Santa isn't real, you sick fuck." I pointed at the mall Santa. "This guy isn't Santa Claus. Neither were any of the other mall Santas you killed."

"You hear that?" Jack lifted Santa's chin. "Captain Obvious here says you're not really Santa Claus."

"That's what I've been trying to tell you! My name is Mac Pelznickel. I live in a trailer with my wife and a puggle we spend way too much money on since our daughter got married. I dress up as Santa to help spread the Christmas Spirit."

"Exactly!" Jack tightened his grip on the knife. The blood from Mac's neck was a steady stream now. "Santa isn't real, but the Christmas Spirit certainly is. I saw a documentary recently interviewing mall Santas. They all said when they put on the costume, the Christmas Spirit takes over their body and, in their minds, they become Santa Claus."

"What does that have to do with this guy, or the other Santas you butchered?" I asked.

"I figured he'd eventually show up to save one of them."

"Show up? You expect Santa to fly down the chimney and rescue this guy?"

Jack shook his head. "Of course not. I know Santa's not a real person. And even if he were, the physics don't work. But the Christmas Spirit is *definitely* real."

"Suppose the Christmas Spirit does show up. What are you gonna do?"

"Kill him."

"Why?"

"Because the Christmas Spirit is total bullshit!" he yelled. "I worked retail for ten years, and let me tell you, everybody only *acts* all nice. Until you're out of the latest over-marketed crap that little Timmy's been crying for, and then the parents turn into fucking Krampuses!"

"Krampi," Mac said. Blood bubbled on his lips.

"What?"

"The plural of Krampus isn't Krampuses. It's Krampi."

"Like a bunch of Elvises are called Elvi?" I asked.

"Exactly." He coughed a spray of blood, then passed out.

"Fine, they turned into a bunch of Krampi!" Jack shoved the knife in deeper. "And they took it out on me. It's not my fault they waited too late to get everything on their rotten little crotch fruit's wish list. But they sure treated me like it was."

"So let me get this straight," I said. "A few shitty parents hurt your feelings when you worked at the department store, so you started torturing and killing mall Santas in order to lure the Spirt of Christmas here so you can have your revenge?"

"It sounds crazy when you say it like that, but pretty much, yeah."

The blood around Mac's severed toes sizzled. Was the coal reigniting?

"There's just one problem," I said.

"What's that?"

"Mac's dead."

"What?" Jack lifted Mac's head. The light had left his eyes.

I glanced at the coals. They were definitely getting hotter.

Jack threw his knife at the overhead light, then lunged for the axe. The knife shattered the bulb, plunging the room into darkness. I shot where I thought Jack had jumped. The flash lit up the room for a split second, enough to see Jack grab his leg and fall over.

"Fuck!" he screamed before his head bounced off the concrete.

As I clicked on my flashlight, the coals caught fire. I cuffed Jack, then kicked the coals away and smothered the flames.

That's when I noticed Mac was glowing.

"The fuck?" I looked back toward the door, praying my backup would burst in and save me.

"Your backup's not coming," Mac said. "Or, rather, they can't come to where we are."

"What do you mean?"

Mac flexed, and the zip ties holding him to the chair snapped.

"I mean, we're in a space-time bubble, separate from your linear timeline. How do you think I deliver all those presents around the world in just one night?"

He stood up, dusted himself off, and straightened his beard. He spit out another tooth.

"Sit back down," I said. I didn't want to take my gun off Jack, but I had a bad feeling about Mac now. His cuts and bruises were healing as I watched.

"Relax, Puddles. I'm not going to hurt you. So far, you've been nothing but nice. Him, on the other hand…" He kicked Jack in the side. "Well, he's been a little naughty."

How did he know about Puddles? Nobody had called me that since Grandma died.

I looked at the foot he'd kicked Jack with. His toes had grown back.

"Are you…?"

"In the flesh." His eyes twinkled. "Well, in Mac's flesh anyway." He crinkled his nose, and the blood disappeared from his face and hair. "I'm only gonna need this body for a few more minutes, then you can have it back. Just thought I'd clean it up a bit. No need for his widow to see him like this. Especially so close to Christmas." He kicked Jack again. "Sorry, you can't have Jack though. He's coming with me."

"Like hell he is." I aimed my gun at Mac. Was I really going to shoot Santa Claus?

"You can't stop me, Puddles. Trust me, he'll get what's coming to him."

"What are you gonna do?"

"He'll work as an elf until he dies, and then get ground into reindeer food. Unless I decide to just feed him to the reindeer tonight. Fresh meat is a rare treat. But first I need to get him down to traveling size."

"Traveling size?"

With a wink of his eye and a twist of his head, Santa made Jack's body fold into itself. Jack's bones broke, shrank, then reset. His ears grew pointy, and whiskers sprouted from his chin. His face froze in a hideous rictus, but I could see the agony in his eyes. I fought the urge to throw up.

Santa wiggled his nose, and Mac's lifeless body fell to the ground. The tree burst into flames, and Jack faded away. His eyes, white and wide with terror, were the last I saw of him.

As my backup finally broke through the door, sleigh bells echoed on the wind.

THE SPACE BETWEEN

"What kind of car is this?" Erik asked as he buckled his seatbelt. "I've never seen anything like it before."

"It's an import," Vaughn, his driver, answered. "Not many of 'em over here yet." He waited for a gap in traffic, then pulled out from the curb.

"So, you a big Corey Hart fan?" Erik asked as they merged onto the freeway a few minutes later.

"Who?"

"You know, because you're wearing your sunglasses at night?"

Vaughn looked at him. He didn't take his sunglasses off though. "I don't get it."

"Never mind."

The trip since had been pretty quiet. Erik had spent most of it with his head against the passenger window, looking up at the stars. It was a clear, moonless night, and the farther they got from the city, the more stars appeared. Erik could still pick out most of the constellations he'd learned in Cub Scouts. He'd wanted to be an astronomer growing up— even had his own telescope—but that changed once he got to college and realized the math was way over his head. The stars still brought him comfort; no matter where life took him—and it had taken him to some awful places over the years—he knew they'd always be up there waiting for him. It was sad to think about, but they were one of the few things left in life he could count on.

"Mind if I play the radio?" Vaughn asked.

Erik lifted his head from the passenger window. "Sure, go ahead. Maybe you'll find an '80s station playing Corey Hart and I won't feel like a total dork."

"Don't worry about it," Vaughn said. He fiddled with the knob for a few minutes, but couldn't find anything he liked. He finally gave up and left it on static, tapping his fingers to a beat Erik couldn't quite pick up.

That's an odd choice, he thought, but decided to let it go. They still had at least six more hours together, depending on gas and pee breaks, and it wasn't worth upsetting his driver. Especially in the middle of the night out here in the middle of nowhere.

"Thanks again for picking me up on such short notice," Erik said instead. "Uber and Lyft both declined my trip. Said it was too long for their drivers. I was about to try the bus station when out of nowhere, your app just popped up on my screen. I don't even remember downloading it, to be honest, but I don't know what I'd have done without it. My girlfriend just dumped me, my cat ran away, even my cactus died. Sometimes I think this world has it out for me." He took a deep breath. "Sorry to unload like that. I just really needed to get the heck out of Dodge, and your app was a real lifesaver."

"Out of Dodge?" Vaughn asked. "What does that mean? I thought you lived in Omaha?"

"You know, out of your present situation, away from something bad? I think it's from *Gunsmoke*. You never saw that show?"

Vaughn shrugged his shoulders. "Guess I missed that one too," he said. "Anyway, I'm glad you needed a ride. I'm always looking for an excuse to get out of the house and back on the road. I was a truck driver for almost thirty years. Semiretired a few years back. I'd fill in on the shorter routes if one of our drivers couldn't make it, but for the most part, I stayed home to take care of my wife. She was pretty sick."

"How's she's doing?"

"She passed last year." He took off his sunglasses and wiped his eyes. "Point is, the app's been a lifesaver for me too."

"Sorry."

"Thanks." Vaughn put his sunglasses back on.

Erik changed the subject. "Almost thirty years, huh? How many states did you hit?"

Vaughn puffed his chest. "Forty-seven of the fifty-three, according to the company logs. But a couple off-the-book side trips got me up to forty-nine. That was before they started chip-tracking us, of course." He patted the dash. "Couldn't get away with that kind of thing these days."

"Don't you mean fifty?"

"What? Oh yeah, fifty. Duh." Vaughn twirled his finger next to his ear. "Old age, I guess. Anyway, I missed being behind the wheel. And I gotta admit, this car's a lot easier to drive than my rig ever was. Cargo's usually nicer too."

Erik smiled. "Thanks."

"One thing I've learned driving folks around is that most people have no idea how big and empty this country of ours really is," Vaughn said. "Especially now that every phone has a WayFinder in it. They just look at the little area displayed on their screens and think that's it. But pull out an actual map sometime and look at how much empty space there is between towns. It's easy to get lost out there in all that space. The space between…" His voice trailed off. "Shoot, listen to me prattle on," he said, shaking his head. "Probably keeping you from updating your MyFace or something. Just tell me to shut up if you want."

"I don't mind," said Erik, and he meant it. Pining over pictures of his ex was the last thing he wanted to do right now. "Bet you saw some weird stuff out there, huh?"

"Stuff you wouldn't believe," Vaughn said.

"Try me."

Vaughn cocked his head, then nodded. "Okay. You know those empty spaces on the map?"

"The space between?"

Vaughn chuckled. "Yeah, those. Here's the thing, Erik. They're not always empty. In fact, sometimes they are chock full of some real crazy stuff. I've seen creatures out there you'll never see on the Animal Channel, skulking in the ditches beside the road, gliding through the trees…"

"Pics or it didn't happen."

Vaughn snickered. "Like I'd get out and selfie myself."

Erik laughed. Listening to Vaughn talk was like listening to his dad trying to sound hip, bless his heart.

Vaughn fiddled with the radio some more, finally stopping on a frequency where faint voices popped and crackled through the static.

"I hear people whispering to me on the radio sometimes," he said. "In the static between stations. One night, I heard my mother talking to me. She'd been dead twenty years at that point. Another time I heard my own voice, begging me not to leave my wife by herself. I laughed it off—couldn't be real, right?—but when I got home late that night, I found her unconscious on the couch. EMTs took her straight to the hospital, but she never woke up." He sighed. "Guess I should've taken my advice, huh?"

Erik's eyes widened. Vaughn couldn't really believe that, could he? Before he could ask, Vaughn changed the subject.

"You know anything about quantum physics, Erik? The multiverse? Schrödinger's rat?"

Erik nodded, glad to be talking about something else. "A little, although I thought it was Schrödinger's cat."

"Tomato, tomahto," Vaughn said.

"It's been a while since college, but if I remember right, scientists think there are an infinite number of universes, right?"

"That's right. All sitting right next to each other." Vaughn pinched his forefinger and thumb as close as he could without touching.

"But scientists also say it's impossible for anything to cross from one to the other, right?"

Vaughn snorted. "Those scientists need to come down out of their ivory towers and get out here with us regular folks, Erik. I'd tell 'em the same thing I'm about to tell you." He paused for effect. "The bigger the open space, the smaller the space between. There are spots along these roads where the space between worlds is so thin it's practically nonexistent. It's easy to cross through there."

A meteor shot across the sky up ahead. They watched it disappear over the hills.

"When I first started driving, there were only a few thin spots like that, and only on the *backest* of the back roads. Truckers knew which ones to avoid. There are lots more now though. And they're spreading out to places beyond the open spaces."

Vaughn had to be messing with him now, right? But since they still had a few hundred miles ahead of them, Erik decided to play along. "Okay, let's say I crossed through one of those thin spots. How would I know?" he asked.

"Just pay attention," Vaughn said. "You'll know."

"Pay attention to what?"

He shrugged. "Big things, little things. Anything, everything." He pointed to Erik's window. "I saw you looking up at the stars earlier," he said. "One night I pulled off the side of the road to take a leak. Sky that night was filled with so many stars it hurt to look at them. But they weren't *my* stars, the ones I learned in Scout Pack. The constellations I grew up with were gone. My *sky* was gone."

Erik waved his hand. "That happens to everyone," he said. "City lights are so bright these days you can't see anything *but* the constellations, so when you get out in the open it can be a little overwhelming. It's even worse if the moon's not out."

"Yeah, like I didn't think of that?" Vaughn snapped. "Sorry. But those weren't my stars." He gripped the wheel as he spoke. "They were all jumbled up. Different colors too. Red, blue, green… I swear some of them were even black, darker than the sky itself. There were two moons too. How do you explain that?"

"Reflection off the clouds? Trick of the atmosphere...?" Erik's voice trailed off.

"That's what I thought too. Until I felt it."

"Felt what?"

"Something out there *behind* those stars. Something looking for me. I got so scared standing out there my bladder froze. Ran back to my rig and got the heck out of Dodge, as you say, before whatever it was found me."

Erik didn't know what to say, so he leaned against the passenger window and looked outside. The Big Dipper was gone. He leaned forward over the dash and looked up through the front windshield. He couldn't find the Little Dipper or Cassiopeia either.

"I've seen pale white figures running alongside the road, keeping pace with my rig," Vaughn said, ignoring Erik's agitated state. "Their skin shimmered in the moonlight as they ran." His voice grew quieter. "Once something so huge walked across the highway ahead of me, all I could see were its legs. The rest of it just disappeared up in the clouds. Ground shook like an earthquake every time it took a step."

Erik was barely listening now. He rolled down his window and stuck his head outside. The wind made his eyes water, but he could see the sky was all wrong.

"Other times, the signs are more subtle," Vaughn said as he slowed down and coasted onto the berm. "Car brands you've never heard of. Maps with the wrong number of states. Or something as simple as a new app on your phone. One you don't even remember downloading."

The car rolled to a stop, its headlights illuminating a sign for the Eris Ridge Trail.

Vaughn killed the engine. "And the people?" He took off his sunglasses. "Well, you don't want to make eye contact; let's leave it at that."

Erik's stomach dropped. He threw open the door and stumbled out of the car, landing on his backside. Gravel and grit ground into his palms as he skittered away from the car. His head tilted back, and he froze. Millions of multicolored stars shimmered overhead, a sea of sinister jewels: endless, brilliant, dizzying in number. But they weren't *his* stars, the ones he'd learned as a child. Erik felt a presence then, something ancient stirring far beyond the stars. It was looking for him. A dark stain spread down the front of his pants.

Vaughn smiled, then reached across the seat and shut the passenger door. The dome light turned off. In the darkness, Vaughn's pupils glowed a sickly orange. He started the car and turned up the radio. Erik heard his own voice breaking through the static, warning him not to use the app.

As Vaughn drove off, the ground began to shake.

THE TUNNEL AT THE END OF
THE LIGHT

"Can anyone tell me why this tunnel was originally built?" asks the man in the bloody banana suit.

They're in a tunnel under the main building of the Stanley Hotel on the second day of a three-day writers' retreat. The tunnel is the last stop on the hotel's ghost tour. Erik wonders if their guide's blood-splattered banana suit is in the spirit of the retreat or just his normal attire.

"Prohibition?" an older woman at the back of the group asks.

"No, but that's a good guess," the guide says, throwing her a finger-gun salute. "They built it so the servants could get around without being seen by the hotel guests."

"You're saying they built it so rich people wouldn't have to look at the poor people who were serving them?" asks the woman's companion.

"Exactamundo." He blows on his finger and holsters it.

"Guess some things never change," Erik says. A few people laugh.

***

Erik had arrived at the hotel on Friday evening. The only other time he'd been to Estes Park was one of the last good memories he had. *Could he handle being there again, considering the way things had gone since?* His job had transferred him from Denver to Menard not long after that visit. Erik hated everything about Texas. The weather was too hot, the chili not hot enough. And the neighbors were downright cold. That small-town Texas hospitality he'd heard so much about was total bullshit. Worst of all, just six months after relocating, he'd had to put down Koko, his black border collie, leaving a Texas-sized hole in his heart that no amount of alcohol could fill.

Dusk had descended as he crossed the bridge over Lake Estes. Dark winter clouds swallowed the tops of the surrounding mountains. Snow blanketed the landscape. In the distance, the hotel seemed to float above the town on a bed of marshmallow fluff. The courtyard lights blinked on, shimmering through the falling snow. Were they welcoming him back? Or luring him in?

***

The hotel had screwed up his reservation and given him a king bed instead of the queen he'd requested. The desk clerk told Erik they wouldn't charge him for the upgrade, but Erik hadn't asked for a smaller bed to save money. He just didn't want to be reminded of how lonely he was. While he'd never shared his bed with someone for more than a night or two, Koko had slept at his side since the day she was house-trained. Now the empty space was another reminder of how much he missed her. This trip was supposed to help him get over that, to move onto the "acceptance" phase of the grieving process, as his therapist said in their last session. He hoped he didn't regret coming.

He tossed his suitcase on the bed and looked around. In addition to the bed, there were two nightstands, a small table and chairs, and a TV sitting atop a dresser. The living area's single small window offered a partial view of the patio's corrugated roof. Not exactly the gothic atmosphere the organizers had promised. He unpacked and headed downstairs.

The lobby was a blur of activity. A long line of guests waited to check in at the front desk. Although the hotel used key cards now, there was a display behind the counter with the original metal keys for each room. A tour guide led a group of visitors through the crowd, pointing out portraits of previous owners as they snaked their way toward the ballroom. Leather chairs and couches were occupied far beyond the recommended seating capacity. A group of people with lanyards matching Erik's chatted next to a massive stone fireplace near the bar entrance. He started toward them. When he saw a man cuddling a small black dog near the front door, Erik's heart sank.

They let dogs in here?

Not long before he moved to Texas, he and Koko had spent a long weekend camping in Rocky Mountain National Park. Since the Stanley was only a few miles away, Erik told Koko they had to check it out. He assumed dogs weren't allowed inside, so they'd shadowed a passing tour group before branching off on their own.

Near the entrance to the concert hall, Koko had perked up. She sniffed around in circles, trying to catch a scent. When she finally locked in on one, she pulled hard at her leash, dragging Erik toward the doorway. He squatted and put his arm around her.

"What is it, Koko?" he whispered into her ear. "Is it the twins?"

She gave him a look as if to say, "Come on, dude, the Grady twins aren't real," then shook off his arm and pulled toward the doorway again. When he wouldn't let her go inside, she lost interest and peed on the flowers.

They walked across the road toward a trail the park ranger had recommended. "When you reach the fork, go left," he'd said. "The right goes to the Eris Ridge Trail. You don't wanna go on that one." Once they'd passed the fork, Erik unclipped her leash and Koko bolted down the path, leaving a cloud of grit and pine needles in her wake. Scrub brush and Ponderosa pines lined the rocky track, and piles of deadfall ensured she couldn't stray too far off course. He followed her happy bark, catching an occasional blur of black as she wound her way down the path. The sun warmed him as he walked. The trail ended with a postcard view of the Rockies, the town a shiny diamond in the valley below. Erik told Koko to sit and took a few pictures with the mountains as a backdrop. He still had one of those shots as the wallpaper on his computer.

A hot, fishy smell snapped him back to reality. The man he'd seen at the far end of the lobby now held his dog about six inches from Erik's face. "Excuse me," the man said, "but Percy told me you looked sad. He's sensitive to these things."

Erik assured Percy he was fine, then headed for the bar.

"Table for one?" the hostess asked. Erik nodded.

"Did you know we have the largest selection of whiskey, bourbon, and scotch in the entire state?" she asked as she led him to his table. She handed him a whiskey menu once he sat down.

"No, thanks." He handed the menu back. "I hate whiskey. Just bring me a local IPA and a grilled cheese sandwich."

He took a Xanax while he waited for his food; fingers crossed that the combo wouldn't haunt his stomach.

***

Erik guessed there'd been thirty to forty other horror writers at the opening ceremonies after dinner. At least two-thirds of them were now crowded into a small one-bedroom condo located up the hill behind the hotel. He recognized several people from their book jackets, but didn't have the nerve to approach them. After a few minutes playing wallflower by the keg (where he downed two more beers), he went out to the patio.

A half-dozen or so attendees huddled near the propane heaters, drinking beers and passing a couple joints around.

While he'd always been socially awkward, he'd withdrawn even more since his move to Texas. He'd hoped his IPA and Xanax dinner cocktail would give him the courage to say hi to the other writers tonight. Instead, it only made his anxiety worse. He slunk into a corner, his breath in the moonlight the only hint of his presence. When he caught himself nodding off for the third time, he went back to the hotel.

Outside his room, he fumbled with his key card. It took three tries to open the door. He'd left the TV on before he went to the party, tuned to the hotel's in-house channel showing Kubrick's version of *The Shining* on a 24-hour loop. He watched Danny run through the hedge maze for a few minutes, then turned the volume down and passed out.

He couldn't remember his dreams this morning, but his pillow was damp with tears.

***

As the guide in the bloody banana suit continues to ramble on about the haves and have-nots, Erik examines the tunnel. The ceiling is roughly seven to eight feet high, depending on where you stand. The dry, dusty air tastes slightly metallic. Floor joists and support beams rest on top of the rock walls. A single bulb hangs from the ceiling. Its feeble glow brings more attention to the places you can't see than those you can.

"Where does that go?" someone asks, pointing to a small opening in the rocks behind the guide.

"Further back into the mountain," the guide says. "We used to let people crawl in there, but we had to stop a couple years ago after a guest went missing."

"What happened?" asks a teenager to Erik's left.

"Guy said he saw his dead mother sitting in the back of the tunnel and crawled in after her. He never came back out."

The guide turns and points his flashlight at a larger opening in the rocks further down the larger tunnel. "That one you can still check out though. Whoever—or whatever—hides back there likes to give out hugs, if you're into that sort of thing."

"Someone really disappeared down here?" Erik asks as the others walk ahead.

The guide shrugs. "I just read the script they give me, man."

Erik hangs back as the group exits the tunnel, halfheartedly hoping for a hug.

***

Later that evening, Erik heads back to the bar.

The bartender points to his lanyard when she delivers his IPA. "You're one of the writers? What's on the agenda tonight?"

Erik takes a long drink before answering. "More of these."

"After that, I mean."

"There is no 'after' when drinking is involved. Especially with us writers. There's just a brief interlude between drinks."

She laughs. It reminds him of happier times with his friends in Denver, before the move. Before he lost Koko. He takes another long swallow, trying to drown the memory.

"You write anything I might have read?" she asks.

"Depends. You like horror stories?"

"Like *Pretty Woman*?"

"What? No, not whore. *Horror.* You know, ghosts, zombies, psycho killers. The things that made this hotel famous?"

"Not me." She shivers. "I hate that stuff."

Erik's shoulders slump. "I'll take another IPA, please."

He pulls the program up on his phone while he waits. The "Death Tunnel Story Hour" is up next. One of the weekend's honorees is reading a story in the tunnel Erik had toured earlier that afternoon. That sounded better than sitting alone at the bar.

The bartender drops off his check with his beer. Erik raises his glass to the mirror in a mock toast. His sad-eyed reflection reluctantly toasts back.

***

The writers slowly work their way into the tunnel. Most of them are wearing jackets and long pants, while Erik and a few other guys sport the standard writer's ensemble of cargo shorts and an ironic t-shirt. He heads for the back corner, where the huggy spirit likes to hang out. Maybe he'll get lucky this time.

The guest of honor walks to the center of the tunnel and stands under the light, waiting for someone to turn it off.

"Now it's dark," he says when the light goes out. The author's face, illuminated by the dim glow of his laptop, floats in the darkness.

Erik chuckles. There's never a bad time for a *Blue Velvet* reference. He leans against the cold stone and closes his eyes. A smile spreads across his face as the alcohol kicks in. He's only half-listening, sinking in the warm embrace of a high-altitude buzz.

Something licks the back of his calf.

He slaps down at his leg and feels a quick brush of fur across the back of his hand. Claws *click-clack* across the stone floor.

"There's something back here!"

He fumbles with his phone, but someone turns on the overhead light before he can hit his flashlight app. Erik spins around, frantically searching the ground around him for paw prints, while the rest of the group stares at him.

The only tracks in the dust are his.

***

After the reading, Erik heads straight back to the bar. A few other writers sit with him.

"Are you sure it was a dog?" asks a blonde he thinks he recognizes.

"I felt its fur."

"It could've been a spider," says her curly-haired boyfriend.

"Yeah, that makes me feel way better," Erik says. "Besides, it licked me. And spiders don't have tongues."

"You sure about that?" asks a bald guy with a goatee and a black widow head tat.

"No, I'm not sure about spider tongues. But I am sure something licked me." He takes a long swig of his beer and pops half a Xanax. He doesn't care if they notice. "And I'm pretty sure it was my dog, Koko."

"Did you bring Koko with you?"

"No," Erik says. "She died last year."

"Sorry." The blonde touches his forearm.

Her boyfriend puts his arm around her. "Obviously it wasn't Koko. Maybe it was that weird guy's dog—"

"Percy?" the guy with the head tat asks.

"Was that the guy's name?"

"No, Percy was his dog's name," Erik says. "And it turns out he's not part of the retreat, so they wouldn't let him down there."

Erik signals the server for another beer.

"Why don't you finish any of your beers? Backwash?" The boyfriend points to the pint glasses in front of Erik's plate. There's a sip left in each of them.

"Force of habit, I guess. Koko loved beer, so I'd always save a little sip for her."

"You let your dog drink beer?" head tat asks.

"Best drinking buddy I ever had. Most responsible too. One time, I'd had a horrible day at work and started drinking as soon as I got home. A few hours into the evening, Koko started spilling my beers. At first I thought she was playing around and wanted to join me, but after the third time I noticed she wasn't drinking any. I think she was telling me I'd had enough." He pauses while the server delivers his pint. "Man, I miss her."

The blonde lifts her glass. "To Koko," she says. Erik and the others return the toast. "To Koko."

A few minutes later, they say their goodnights and leave Erik by himself. He knows they don't believe Koko was in the tunnel, but he doesn't care. He's sure Koko had been down there. Two more beers and the second half of his Xanax later, he isn't sure if *he'd* been in the tunnel, let alone his dead dog.

While he waits for the server to bring his check, he notices the others all left a teeny sip for Koko. He wipes away a tear and pays his tab.

Back in his room, he turns on the TV in time to see Jack exchanging pleasantries with Lloyd at the bar. He sprawls across the bed and passes out.

***

A familiar canine whimper yanks Erik back to consciousness.

He sits up and rubs his eyes. The clock reads 3:15 a.m. He must have been dreaming about Koko again.

Koko was just eight weeks old when someone dumped her at the no-kill shelter where he used to volunteer, barely old enough for solid food. Erik fell in love with her the first time she licked his nose. She followed him everywhere, and they'd been inseparable for seventeen years. The last few months of her life had been rough though. She'd lose her bearings at night, whining and barking at things that weren't there, and gradually lost control of her bowels. Doggy Alzheimer's, the vet called it.

Doggy Hell was more like it.

Erik slept on the couch so he'd hear her when she became disoriented. He'd sit on the floor and hold her until she calmed down and went back to sleep.

Another whimper comes from out in the hall. He jumps from the bed and runs out of the room. The door clicks shut behind him. A second later, he realizes he doesn't have his keycard.

Shit.

He'll have to go down to the lobby to get a replacement. Awesome. He hopes none of the other writers are down there.

At the top of the stairs, a familiar jingle floats up from the lobby below. Koko's collar! He'd know the sound her tags made anywhere. He'd ordered them special for her tenth birthday. Erik takes the stairs two at a time and jumps the last three. His ankle buckles when he lands and he tumbles into the darkened lobby. The only light comes from a small lamp at the check-in desk.

Why aren't there more lights on?

The check-in desk is empty. He rings the counter bell and looks around. "Hello?" He rings it a second time, then a third. "Anybody here?" Nobody answers. He wonders if the old metal keys still work. Before he can climb over the counter to grab the one for his room, another jingle echoes out from the direction of the bar. This time he *knows* it's Koko. Still, he hesitates. That end of the lobby is a black hole. Even the embers in the fireplace have died out. He sighs and grabs a book of matches from a bowl on the counter. He lights one and inches his way into the darkness. Four matches and two errant furniture kicks later, he stands at the entrance to the bar.

A happy bark, this time from inside the bar. He expects the door to be locked, but tries it anyway. The handle turns and the door swings open.

"Hello?" No answer.

He lights another match and walks in.

The darkness is complete, a physical presence that flattens his lungs as he searches for a light switch. He finally finds one that controls the small pendant lights hanging over the bar and each booth. It isn't much, but it allows him to move around without tripping over anything. He uses the last of his matches to check under each booth and table. The place is empty, just like the lobby.

Erik slides onto a stool and lays his head down on the bar. His fingers reek of sulfur. His ankle hurts. His heart hurts more. Of course she isn't there. Hell, he'd been holding her in his lap when the vet gave her the final injection. He'd felt her lungs deflate as she expelled her last breath. He'd watched the light in her eyes fade away. What the fuck was he doing stomping around in the dark chasing after his dead dog? How had his life reached this point?

"Evening, sir," a deep male voice asks. "What are we drinking tonight?"

Erik lifts his head. The bar was empty when he came in. He was sure of it. But someone's here now. And that someone is offering him a drink.

"Evening, Lloyd," he says.

The bartender smirks. Clearly, Erik isn't the first guest to make that joke. He wonders if he was the first to come down in the middle of the night looking for their dead dog.

"You haven't seen a dog down here tonight, have you? Black border collie, about thirty-five pounds? Jingly red collar?"

"Sorry, sir, no dogs in here tonight."

"That's okay. I'm sure I just imagined it." Eric drums his fingers on the wooden bar. "Well, since you asked, wanna grab me an IPA?"

"Certainly, sir."

Erik studies his reflection in the bar back mirror while he waits. He barely recognizes the person looking back.

The bartender returns with Erik's beer and sets the pint down.

"Lloyd, it appears I've left my wallet in my room." Erik pats his pockets. "Problem is, I left my keycard up there too. Think you can help me out?"

"No charge to you, sir."

Erik squints at the bartender. "Come again?"

"Your money's no good here, sir," he says, wiping the bar.

"From the book, I get it." Erik chuckles. "That's awesome." He takes a long swig. "How about another one then? Charge it to my room, and give yourself a nice, fat tip. But not too fat. I'm not quite as successful as some of the other writers here this weekend." He sighs. "Hell, compared to them, I'm barely a writer at all."

"I appreciate it, sir. But your drinks are on *him* tonight."

He points to a booth in the far corner of the room. Erik turns. A man sits there, sipping a martini. *What the fuck?* He knows the man wasn't there a moment ago. Just like Lloyd hadn't been—until he was. If this is a dream, at least his subconscious is keeping it interesting.

The man motions for Erik to join him. Erik's stomach tightens.

"Go on," says the bartender. "He doesn't bite. I'll see what I can do about your key."

"Thanks." Erik takes a deep breath and runs his hands through his hair. He picks up his beer and walks toward the booth. The temperature drops with each step.

"Thanks for the beer, buddy." He stands at the edge of the booth and tries to avoid eye contact. "You haven't seen a dog around here, have you?"

The man shakes his head. He's slender, with black, wavy hair, and a neatly trimmed beard. Dark suit, no tie. He points to the open seat.

"I must have imagined it." Erik hesitates, then sits. "This place, it'll do that to you, right?" He raises his glass. "Anyway, cheers to you."

The man raises his glass in return.

"Not the talkative type, huh?" Erik asks. "That's okay. I'm used to it. Transferred to a new office and my coworkers haven't exactly gone out of their way to welcome me. Neighbors flat out ignore me. I just talk to my dog Koko." He pauses. "Well, I did, before…" He spins the pint glass between his hands and stares at the beer.

The pendant light above their table buzzes and flicks off. When it comes back on, the man's features have changed.

His hair is longer, his beard bushier. His nose (*snout?*) more pronounced.

Flick.

The man's suit is gone, replaced by a black t-shirt with a lightning bolt and the words *"Lick 'Em All, Let Dog Sort Them Out"* emblazoned across the front. His arms are covered in fur, a black claw at the end of each finger. He smiles, revealing impossibly long canine teeth.

Erik jumps out of his seat.

Flick.

The man, normal again. His arms shoot across the table. Cold, dry hands swallow Erik's and pull him back down. On the back of his right hand is a tattoo of a German shepherd. As Erik struggles to break free, the tattoo ripples and runs across to his other hand.

The air has grown so cold Erik can see his breath. He can also see that the other man isn't breathing.

"What the hell?"

Flick.

Erik is back in the vet's office, cradling Koko's head in his lap as the vet administers the second shot. "You can stay with her as long as you need to," she says.

"It's going to be okay," he tells Koko, stroking her head. "It won't hurt anymore when you walk, and every day will be sunny and warm. I'll see you again soon, I promise."

Her breathing slows, and she looks up toward an empty corner of the room. She cocks her head, puzzled, and seems to relax. He tells Koko it's okay to go. Koko's tail wags one last time, her lungs deflate, eyes glass over, and she's gone. Erik wails. He strokes her head, rocking and sobbing and cradling the loose bag of bones that moments before had been his best friend.

Sometime later—he doesn't know how long—he kisses Koko's forehead and rubs behind her ears one last time. He stands and leaves her on the floor. He can barely see through the tears.

Flick.

Erik is back in the booth, teeth chattering, fingers numb. "What the hell?" He jerks again, harder this time, but can't pull free.

"Lloyd! Help!"

He looks over his shoulder at the empty bar.

The man squeezes Erik's hands together and pulls him closer.

Flick.

Erik is back in the vet's office, this time watching from a spot in the corner, about six feet above the floor. From this new vantage point, he can see himself sitting on the floor, cradling Koko's head in his lap. She looks up at him, cocks her head, wags her tail one last time, and draws her final breath.

Erik sees himself crying, rocking back and forth. And then he sees Koko's spirit leave her body. She steps away from Erik and trots over to the corner where he's watching from now—the same corner she'd been so interested in right before she died. A hand reaches down, but it's not his. It's pale, with a German shepherd tattoo. It rubs Koko behind the ears. Her tail wags, and she gives the hand a quick, wet lick. She looks back at Erik, still sitting across the room and crying over her lifeless body. She walks over and barks at him, trying to get his attention. He doesn't notice. She lets out a little whine and tilts her head, puzzled, as he continues to ignore her. Erik stands and walks out of the room, leaving Koko behind...

Flick.

The man releases Erik's hands and leans back in his seat. "Were you... *there?*" Erik asks. "Was I seeing what you saw?"

The man nods. *"I'm always there."* His ancient voice echoes inside Erik's head. *"To guide the ones who are ready to go."* He snaps his fingers. Koko jumps into the booth with him. *"And help the ones who aren't."*

Flick.

***

Erik rolls over and looks at the clock. 12:30 p.m. He sits up and rubs the sleep from his eyes. *What the fuck happened last night?* It seemed so real, but it had to have been a dream, right? He'd drank too much beer and taken too many pills. Of course it was a dream.

Wasn't it?

He swings his legs over the side of the bed, but winces in pain when his foot touches the floor. His ankle is purple and swollen.

***

The final scheduled activity of the retreat is a late-night paranormal investigation led by a local ghost hunter. The pain in Erik's ankle has progressed from dull ache to deep throb over the afternoon. He's exhausted and can't stay focused, but no way he is missing this, so he sucks it up and drags himself down to the ballroom to wait with the other writers.

The ghost hunter arrives a few minutes later and thanks everyone for coming. After a brief introduction covering his background and the equipment he brought, he leads them down to the tunnel. The group forms a loose circle under the tunnel's only light. This time Erik ends up near the smaller tunnel the tour guide said had been closed to the public.

"We're going to do an EVP session now," the investigator says. "EVP stands for 'Electronic Voice Phenomenon.' Some people believe spirits communicate at a level or frequency we might not hear with our ears but can be picked up on the recorder. We'll take turns asking the spirits questions. After each question, I need everyone to be quiet for a few moments, to give the spirits a chance to answer. Then the next person can ask their question. When everyone's had a chance to ask something, I'll rewind the tape and see if we picked anything up." He turns on the recorder and turns off the light.

The first person asks their question. "Are you here?"

Pause.

"Are you happy?"

Pause.

"Do you miss being alive?"

Pause.

Erik can't believe how stupid their questions are. A once-in-a-lifetime chance to talk with a ghost at one of the world's most haunted hotels, and "Are you here?" is the best anyone can come up with?

Finally, it's his turn.

"Koko?"

Someone stifles a giggle.

Okay, so maybe his wasn't the best question either. But after everything he'd been through this weekend, he feels he deserves an answer.

The guide rewinds the recorder and starts the playback.

The recorded voices are distant and hollow in the dead air of the tunnel. A couple times someone thinks maybe they hear something on the tape, but there's nothing anyone can agree on.

"Koko?" Erik's recorded voice sounds small and lost.

But instead of the fuzzy ambient hum he expects to hear, there's a bark, followed by the sound of happy panting and the familiar jingle of Koko's collar.

"Holy shit!" Erik says. "Did you hear that? That's my dog! Play it again!"

The investigator rewinds the tape and replays the exchange.

"Koko?" he hears himself ask. Koko answers.

Erik fumbles for his phone and drops it in the darkness. It bounces in the dirt behind him. He reaches down and starts feeling around on the ground for it. A warm, wet lick runs up the back of his hand.

"Someone turn on the light! Koko's here in the tunnel!" Erik knows he sounds frantic, but he doesn't care. She's really here this time!

He's on his knees, crawling blindly through the dark, searching for his phone. He hits his head on a rock, hard. Stars explode across his vision, and he falls to his elbows. The tunnel light comes on, and he sees his phone laying facedown a foot or so inside the smaller tunnel. He crawls in, grabs his phone, and turns on the flashlight app.

Koko is sitting a few feet further back, grinning her happiest doggie grin. She looks at Erik, her once-dead eyes now sparkling and full of life. She barks once, then turns and disappears into the dark.

Eric looks back over his shoulder, into the larger area behind him. The others stare down at him, their expressions a mix of shock and apprehension.

"It's okay," he says. "It's Koko!"

The ghost hunter squats down and touches Erik's foot. "Speaking as a professional, you should *not* go in there, man. This place, it's…"

Erik sighs. "I know. But she's my dog. And I miss her." He crawls further into the tunnel. Within a few feet, total darkness envelops him. He looks back. There's no light behind him anymore.

A happy bark echoes from somewhere up ahead.

Koko.

His phone dims as he crawls. When it finally dies, he tosses it aside and continues forward anyhow, following the jingle of Koko's collar into the void.

A *whoosh* of air is his only warning that something is barreling toward him. A ball of fur hits him full force and knocks him into the tunnel wall. Koko licks his face again and again while he hugs her so tightly it hurts. He leans against the wall and she puts her head in his lap. He doesn't know how long they sit together, but eventually Koko stands up. She nuzzles his hand and pulls at his fingers. It's time.

"Okay, Koko. I'm ready," he says. "Let's go."

They set off into the darkness. Together.

Forever.

NECROPHILIACS ANONYMOUS

"Hello, my name is Paul, and I'm a necrophiliac." He took a deep breath and wiped a small bead of perspiration from his forehead.

"Hi, Paul," the other members of the group answered. There were the regulars: Keith, the de facto leader who wouldn't look out of place on a used car lot; Nancy, a buxom redhead; Thomas, who looked every bit the mortician his father had raised him to be; and Vicki, a spiky-haired EMT. There was also a newcomer who had yet to introduce himself.

"Um, most of you know I've been struggling with the fifth step: admitting to God, to ourselves, and to another human being, the exact nature of our wrongs." Paul wiped away another bead of sweat. "It's just really hard to admit to someone outside this group the exact nature of my wrongs." He lowered his voice. "Especially when I'm not so sure they're wrong."

"Come on, Paul, you know what we do is wrong," said Nancy.

"Is it, though? I mean, sure, 'the man' says it's wrong. That we're not 'supposed' to have sex with dead people." He used air quotes as he spoke. "But come on, do any of you feel wrong when you're doing it?" He looked at each member of the group. Only Thomas would meet his gaze.

"Paul, we've gone over this before," Thomas said. "There's no need to make us feel any guiltier than we already do. That's why we're all here. Because we know it's wrong, and we need help to control our addiction before it hurts anyone else."

"But who does it hurt, really? I mean—"

"Okay, that's enough." Vicki cut him off. "You said you wanted to talk about step five. So talk about step five. Did you find someone to admit the exact nature of your wrongs to?"

"Actually, I did." Paul smiled. "I know, hard to believe, right? Her name is Joanie. We met at work. I could tell right away that there was something special about her. I don't know if it was her kind face, the way she didn't interrupt me when I was talking…" He looked directly at Vicki. "Or maybe it was all just chemical. But I knew I could trust her the moment I laid eyes on her. And that she wouldn't judge me. In fact, I think she might have been a little turned on by the whole thing. Because later that night, we got to bumping uglies."

"Wait a minute," said Keith. "You said you met her at work?"

"Yeah."

"And she never interrupted you?" asked Vicki.

"Nope."

"Jesus, Paul, she's dead, isn't she?" Nancy rubbed her forehead.

"Step five doesn't say it has to be a living person."

"Of course it has to be a living person, you moron," Vicki said. "What's the point otherwise?"

Thomas let out an exasperated sigh, then leaned over to the newcomer. "Paul works in the morgue at a local hospital," he said.

Paul shrugged. "Guys, I'm sorry, okay? But if you would've seen her... I know you'd have done it, Keith. You too, Vicki. She was just your type."

"What, gay?"

"No, dead."

"Oh, fuck me." Nancy threw her arms in the air.

Paul smiled at her. "Not while you're still breathing."

"Enough!" Keith shouted. "Paul, you've had your fun. Now sit down and let someone talk who actually wants our help. What about you, Thomas? You look like you have something you need to get off your chest."

"Actually, I do," Thomas said. "Thanks." He cleared his throat. "Hi, my name is Thomas, and I'm a necrophiliac."

"Hi, Thomas," the group answered.

"Well, as you all know, like Paul, my work can be a bit problematic for my addiction." He turned to the newcomer. "I own a mortuary." The newcomer nodded in understanding. "But it's my family's business. My grandfather started it, who passed it down to my father, who passed it down to me. I can't just quit. Unlike Paul." He glared at Paul for a moment. "My employees depend on me. This town depends on me." He looked down at the ground. "But last weekend, I almost got caught with Mrs. Bronson."

"The cashier at the flower shop?" asked Paul.

"That's the one."

"Nice."

"No, Paul, it's not nice. That's the point."

"It felt nice though, didn't it?"

Thomas blushed.

"So what happened?" asked Nancy.

"I tried so hard," Thomas said. "I really did. But at one point I had to roll her over on her side, and something about the way she looked... I just snapped. The next thing I know, I had her bent over the table and I..." He choked back a sob.

Vicki patted him on the knee. "It's okay, keep going."

"When I was...finished, I put her back on the table. Not five seconds later, my assistant walked in. I was mortified. I was so sweaty and frazzled. I hadn't even zipped up yet."

"So did they say anything?" Keith asked.

"Just wanted to know if I needed any help. I told her I thought I was catching a cold, so she should probably let me finish on my own."

Paul snickered. "You'd already finished, dude."

Keith looked at Paul. "Just stop, okay?" He turned back to Thomas. "That had to be scary."

"Terrifying." Thomas wiped a tear away. "I'd been doing so well too. I'd just hit six months."

"Don't beat yourself up, Thomas," Vicki said. "We've all been there. Just remember to take it one day at a time."

Thomas sniffled. "You're right. Thanks, everyone."

The group sat still for a moment, digesting Thomas' story. Then Nancy cleared her throat. "I've got something I'd like to talk about," she said.

"The floor is yours," said Keith.

"Okay. Hi, everyone, my name is Nancy."

"Hi, Nancy."

"You all know I'm a night nurse at the retirement home outside of town, right? Well, sometimes, late at night, it gets real quiet. And since we've had to slash our staff down to the bone because of budget cuts, it can get a little lonely too. Last Thursday night, it was just me and one other worker. She must've got food poisoning or something, because she was throwing up something awful. And I hate the sound of someone throwing up." She shivered. "So I told her to take one of the empty rooms at the end of the hall and try to get some rest. I'd call her if I needed anything. It was pretty quiet until around 4:00 am, when Mr. Ridley died."

"Mr. Ridley, the old insurance guy?" Keith asked.

"That's him. His daughter runs the business now."

"I got my car insurance from him," said Vicki. "Nice guy."

"Nice looking too," said Nancy. "For his age."

"And for being dead," said Paul.

Nancy smiled. "That too." She waited a beat, then continued. "Anyway, you guys remember my cousin Bee? She's come here with me a couple times."

Everyone nodded.

"Well, her family has a mortuary over in Frazier. And she shares the same...appetites...as I do. As we all do. I don't know, maybe it runs in the family? Well, the last time she was here, she gave me a bottle of this special serum she'd been working on. Said she got the idea from someone named Abdul Alhazred? Does that name mean anything to anyone? Not even you, Thomas? I thought maybe since you were both morticians...? Oh well, it doesn't matter. The point is, this serum reanimates whatever part of the body it's injected into."

"Wait, you didn't...?" asked Paul.

"Oh, I did." Nancy tilted her head back and sighed. "And it was fucking amazing! I mean, I've done things with dead guys at work before, obviously. Usually, though, it's just using their hand to help me rub one out. But with Mr. Ridley, this was actual penetrative sex. I don't know what's in that stuff Bee gave me, but it puts Viagra to shame."

"You don't seem very upset about relapsing," said Keith.

She thought for a moment. "You know what? I don't think I am. Why should I be?"

Thomas' jaw dropped. "Because it's wrong?"

"Is it though? I'm beginning to think Paul has a point."

"I do?"

"Yeah, maybe we're looking at this all wrong," she said. "I mean, who does it hurt, really? Sure, they're dead, but they make us feel so alive. I tell you, grinding away on Mr. Ridley's reanimated dick is the most alive I've felt in years."

"You think I could get any of that serum?" Vicki asked.

"Wait, I thought you were into chicks," said Paul.

"No, you assumed I was because I wasn't into you, dumbass. I mainly stick with women, but I've been known to ride the disco stick on occasion, as Lady Gaga says. And this will be so much better than being with a live guy. I won't have to listen to him talk, or feel his gross-ass stubble on my thighs."

"Wait, why is his ass on your thighs?" Paul asked.

"Okay, we can stop it there," said Keith. "Paul, Nancy, I'll concede that maybe, *maybe*, you have a point."

"We do?" asked Paul.

"No, they don't," Thomas said.

Keith rubbed his forehead in frustration. "I said maybe, Thomas. But is this really the look we want to present to our visitor?" He turned to the newcomer. "Would you like to talk?"

"Actually, I would. Thanks," he said. "Hi, my name is Ryan."

"Hi, Ryan," the group answered.

"Well, this is a little awkward, but—"

"I have a question first." Nancy interrupted. "How did you hear about us?"

Ryan looked confused. "I told Keith earlier that Lisa told me about the group. Wait, was she not supposed to?"

The group looked at Keith. "Well, that depends," he said. "Obviously, we try to vet people before we invite them. But I figure if Lisa told you about us, then she must trust you."

"So how do you know Lisa?" Nancy asked.

"I had her for dinner last night."

"Hey, where is Lisa, by the way?" Vicki looked around the room. "It's not like her to miss group."

"Do you mean you had her *over* for dinner last night?" Nancy's eyes narrowed.

"No, I meant what I said. I had her for dinner last night."

Paul pointed at Ryan. "Wait, you're a cannibal?"

"Well, duh."

Keith leapt to his feet. "Get the fuck out of here!"

Ryan's eyes widened. "What? Why? I thought you, of all people, would understand."

"Understand? You defiled a dead body, you sicko!" Nancy yelled.

"Yeah, we have standards," said Thomas.

"Dammit, I wanted to eat Lisa after she died," said Paul.

Keith looked at him. "Wait, you're a cannibal now too?"

"No, but I wanted to *eat* Lisa," Paul said.

"Nice," said Vicki.

Ryan put his hands up and began backing toward the door. "Okay, okay, I'm sorry. I'm leaving now, just—"

BAM! Ryan crumpled to the floor. Nancy stood over him, bits of gore dripping from the fire extinguisher in her hand. Blood from Ryan's cracked skull seeped onto the linoleum.

Keith felt for a pulse. He shook his head. "Shit, Nancy, I think you killed him."

Thomas ran his fingers through his hair as he paced around the room. "Fuck, what should we do with the body? I guess I can take it to the mortuary and cremate it...?"

"I got a better idea." Vicki grinned. "Nancy, you got any of that serum left...?"

MEAT CUTE

Stop staring at her tits!

I knew it was wrong, but I couldn't help myself. It had been so long since I'd had a woman over for dinner. Hell, who was I kidding? It'd been ages since I'd had a woman over for *anything*. And now I was going to ruin it all because I couldn't keep my eyes off her plump, beautiful, perfect breasts.

We'd met earlier that week at the bookstore down the street from my apartment. She was looking at a book on tapas; I was looking for anything to break me out of my rut. A man can only eat his mother's leftovers for so long. When we both reached for the same book, our fingers brushed, and before I knew what I was doing, I asked her out for coffee.

"It, it doesn't have to be a date, not if you don't want it to be," I stammered. "It's just that, well, we both seemed to like the same book. I just thought maybe we could swap recipes."

Swap recipes? Did I really just propose a recipe swap with this woman? Jesus, my mother was right. I am a loser.

I could feel myself dying in front of her.

"I'm not a creep or anything." My eyes dropped, my head followed.

Good one! My father's voice this time, laughing inside my head. *That doesn't make you sound creepy at all.*

"You can bring a friend, if you want," I said, lowering my voice. "You know, if it'd make you feel more comfortable."

"Don't be silly," she said. "I'd love to." She wrote her number on a scrap of paper from her purse and walked out the door.

We had coffee twice that week before I finally got the nerve to ask her over for dinner. She said yes right away.

***

So tonight is the big night. And here we are, in my kitchen, and I *literally* cannot stop staring at her tits. God, could I be any more obvious? I wouldn't be surprised if I were drooling.

She doesn't seem to mind, though. She just looks back at me with a "come hither" expression.

Come hither? I sound like a Harlequin romance.

She continues to look at me, unblinking.

Maybe she wants me to look at them. Maybe she wants me to touch them, to run my hands and lips and tongue over them. To taste *them. To taste her.*

I stopped myself. I had to. Just the thought of her taste on my tongue sent blood rushing to my face, along with other parts of my anatomy. If I didn't stop now, the evening might be ruined. So would my pants.

Shit! Too late.

"I'm sorry," I said, shutting the drawer containing her breasts. I grabbed a piece of thigh from the shelf next to her head, and closed the freezer door.

BLIND SPOT

A dull ache, somewhere near my left eye, pulls me from my sleep. I open my eyes and gag as a wave of nausea rolls over me. I close my eyes again and wait for it to pass. When I'm fairly certain I won't throw up, I try to rub my head, but my arms won't move. I slowly reopen my eyes, one at a time. The room isn't spinning quite as fast this time. A groan escapes me as I realize I'm duct taped to a chair.

Not again.

How much did I drink last night? The last thing I remember is walking to my car after the show. The room had been half-empty, just like the bottle waiting backstage. Turns out there's nothing magical about Monday night at an Omaha mall, even for a magician whose best tricks were of the mental variety: reading minds, guessing cards, that sort of thing. On the coasts, the crowds want bigger, weirder Criss Angel shit, but here in the Heartland, the rubes eat that mentalist crap up. Of course, I'm pretty good at making things disappear too: vodka and an Oxy before the show; an occasional rabbit during, depending on the crowd; and, on a good night, more vodka and the unmentionables of a fan or two afterward. On a bad night, just more vodka.

Clearly, it had not been a good night. While this wasn't the first time I'd awakened strapped to a chair, it was the first I couldn't remember enthusiastically agreeing to beforehand.

The air is damp, with a vague chemical smell. Dust motes dance in a beam of light coming from a window somewhere above and behind me. A basement? A dressing mirror leans against the wall in front of me. The picture it reflects is a far cry from my publicity poster. A golf ball-sized knot above my left eye looks ready to burst. Feels like it too. My jacket and tie are gone. Blood and vomit ribbon down my shirt, a topographic map of pain and bodily fluids. An angry cut runs from my temple down to the corner of my mouth. That's going to leave a killer scar.

Maybe I should rephrase that.

I try rocking the chair back and forth, then side to side, but the damn thing won't move. Who the hell fastens a chair to the floor? And why?

"HELP!" *Shit!* My skull feels like someone fucked it with an icepick. The room spins again. I ignore it. "Hello? Is anyone there?" I say it softer this time, but the pain still makes my eyes water.

Silence.

Fuck it. I have to get out of here. I'll deal with the headache later. "HEL—"

"Don't waste your breath." A woman's voice. I catch a glimpse of her in the mirror before she disappears into the darkness.

***

Too afraid to move, I sit still and try to keep my wits about me. Unfortunately, my wits have plans of their own and have gathered en masse in the vicinity of my sphincter.

What if she doesn't come back?

Don't be an idiot, I tell myself. Of course she'll come back. Why knock someone out and duct tape them to a chair in a cellar if all you're going to do is starve them to death? Even by my showman standards, that's a lot of setup for such an anticlimactic payoff.

What if she brings back someone bigger and badder with a penchant for power tools?

Okay, that could be a problem.

What if she wakes up the gimp? Even worse, what if I'm the gimp?

Maybe starving to death wouldn't be so bad after all.

If I could just get a hand free—and it's a big *if*—is there anything in the basement I could use? For the first time in my career, I regret not adding more escape tricks to my act. I look around. Patches of mold spider up the cinderblock walls. In the corner to my left are a few flattened cardboard boxes and a pile of clothes and shoes; a handful of newspapers and magazines lay scattered in the other. The mirror shows a large wooden cabinet about six feet directly behind me. Glass jars and bottles of various shapes and sizes line each shelf.

I don't want to know what's floating in them.

A low, painful groan breaks the silence. I whip my head from side to side but can't see anything. The effort makes me dizzy, and I close my eyes for a moment. The sound of ragged, wet breathing—sharp intakes of air and slow phlegmy exhalations, punctuated by the smell of rotten meat—brings me closer to panic, but I fight it down. Claws click across the cement floor as something paces in the darkness behind me.

Is it a dog? What's wrong with it? Has she tortured it? Isn't that how serial killers get their start? Should I call out to it? What if it tries to bite me?

I freeze, unable to decide. The panting grows louder.

"You woke Mancha." It's the woman again. Has she been watching me all this time?

"W-w-what?"

She finally walks out to where I can see her. She opens a folding metal chair and sits down a few feet away.

"I said you woke Mancha." She snaps her fingers and whistles. "Come here, boy. Meet The Amazing Andy, the Man with the Magic Eye."

Mancha crawls out of the darkness.

I scream.

Mancha, an average sized beagle with short hair and floppy black ears, gives me a puzzled look. His left eye has two pupils; where his right should be is an empty socket. His tail wags, while a second, broken one spasms and twitches, tracing small sad shapes in the dust. A fifth leg, shriveled and black, hangs uselessly from his side. Every inhalation through Mancha's nose is followed by a foul wet out-breath from a second mouth in his chest. This lower mouth is lined with rows of needle-like teeth.

My eyes bulge as Mancha shuffles closer, his useless second tail flopping behind him. He opens his mouths—the smaller mirrors the movements of the larger—and licks my toes. It's all I can do not to scream again. After a few seconds, Mancha sets his head down atop my foot and goes to sleep.

"Mancha seems to like you," she says. "That's good."

I gasp. "What the hell's wrong with him?"

She bends down and rubs Mancha's head, ignoring my question. "I know he's not much to look at these days, but he's still a good boy."

The dog's important to her. Maybe I can use that. I catalogue details about her appearance as I would before a reading, searching for something, anything, useful. She's average looking, with a plain face. Thirty, maybe thirty-five years old. Mousey brown hair pulled back into a ponytail. Average height and weight. Short, unpolished fingernails. No jewelry. I know I've seen her somewhere before, but can't place where, an itch I can't scratch. It must be the knot on my head. Memory's one of the strongest tricks in my bag, and my recall for faces is usually impeccable.

"Who are you?"

"It doesn't matter who I am." Her voice is quiet, nondescript. "What matters is what I can do."

I flinch as she reaches over and brushes the hair back from my cut. "I'm sorry about that," she says. "You're a lot heavier than you look. I dropped you down the last few steps. You should join a gym."

"That's a great idea," I say. "If you let me go, I promise I'll sign up as soon as I get home. I'll even get myself a personal trainer." I try to smile, but it feels toothy and forced. "I'd cross my heart, but my hands..." I shrug. "Also, I don't hope to die."

She smiles a sad, crooked smile that never touches her eyes. She leans forward and pats my knee, a gesture I might have considered friendly, even flirtatious, under different circumstances. "Maybe we can talk about it after we're finished here," she says.

My heart jumps. "You mean you're not going to kill me?"

"Of course not! Why would you even think such a thing?"

I look around at the room, then down at my hands and feet.

"Fair enough. I can see where it's a little confusing."

"Then what are you going to do to me?"

She looks away.

I lower my voice. "Is it...going to hurt?"

"I hope not."

Cold sweat runs down my back. "What do you mean?"

She ignores my question. "Have you ever thought about your blind spot, Andy? Technically, it's the point where the optic nerve enters your eyeball. Since it doesn't have any rods or cones that respond to light, any image that falls on that spot disappears from sight. Hence the name blind spot." She shines a small flashlight into my left eye, then my right. She clicks off the light and continues. "Everyone with a properly functioning eyeball has one. Well, two, really, since there's one in each eye."

I blink rapidly, trying to clear the stars from my eyes.

"You also have a figurative blind spot, where the things you don't pay attention to disappear." A shadow passes over her face. "I fall into that blind spot with most people. Especially men like you."

I try to look sorry.

"Don't worry," she says. "I'm used to it." I know she's lying. "I'm plain looking. I wear boring clothes. I'm the kind of girl you see, but never *really* see." She laughs, a sharp, bitter sound. "How do you think I got you down here last night?"

"Were you at my show?"

She pulls out a program. "Don't you remember? I was the only one who stayed to get your autograph. I even asked if you'd used the Balducci maneuver on your last card trick. You ignored my question and scribbled your name." She holds up the cover for me to see, then reads the inscription. "'I'll be seeing you! The Amazing Andy.' And you dotted the 'i' in 'Amazing' with a little cartoon eye. Cute."

I flash my best showman's smile. Fewer teeth, more sincerity.

"I'm surprised your magic eye didn't warn you about me," she says, then tosses the program to the floor.

"I hate to break it to you, but I don't really have a magic eye. It's just an act."

"I know, Andy. I'm not an idiot. But I have one." She taps the corner of her right eye. It's the same mousy shade of brown as her hair. "Mine can't see into the future or read minds, but it can make things disappear." She laughs. "I know, it sounds crazy."

"No, it doesn't."

"It doesn't?"

"No, it sounds BATSHIT INSANE! Nobody can make something really disappear. Trust me, I know."

This makes her laugh even harder.

I can't take it any longer. "Who are you?" I shout. The veins in my neck pop as I strain against my bonds. "Where are we? What are you going to do to me?"

"Well, aren't you just a little chatty Kathy all of a sudden." Her eyes narrow. "To answer your first question, my name is Annie. And I'm your number one fan."

Oh shit.

"Sorry, I'm just playing with you," she says with a grin that's instantly forgettable. "My name really is Annie, but I'd never heard of you until I saw your poster in the mall last week. And based on your act, someone *would* have to be crazy to be your fan. Your misdirection was pathetic. Your card forces were beyond blatant. And your mind-reading tricks were total amateur hour. I've seen better craft at a five-year-old's birthday party."

She walks behind me and squeezes my shoulders. "To answer your second question, we're about twenty miles outside Omaha, on a small farm with no neighbors within earshot. That's why I don't care if you scream. And as for what I'm going to do to you," she leans in and whispers, "I'm going to show you the world's greatest magic trick."

"What are you talking about?"

"Haven't you figured it out yet, Andy? I'm going to make *you* disappear."

With a renewed burst of energy, I try to free myself, bouncing in my chair and straining against the tape until it cuts into my flesh. I try screaming, but stop when Mancha's tiny mouth howls along, a high-pitched sound that cuts like a dentist's drill.

When I finish, Annie crosses back in front of me. "Feel better?"

"Not particularly."

"Well then, maybe some magic will cheer you up. Are you ready?"

"Do I have a choice?"

"Not really."

"Will you let me go after you show me your little trick?"

Annie nods.

"Promise?"

Annie sighs. "Yes."

"Then I guess I'm ready. Let's see it."

"Let's *see* it." She claps her hands. "Oh, Andy, that's rich."

"You could be rich if you let me go." I look around the basement. "Well, at least a little better off than you are now. I might play the mall circuit, but I've stashed away a lot of cash over the years. More than enough to get you off this farm. I'll even give you a cut of my next tour."

She sighs. "I don't need your money, Andy. But I do need a volunteer from the audience."

I stare at her. "Really?"

She looks around the room, then down at me. "Looks like we have a volunteer right up here in front! What's your name, sir?"

I don't answer.

"Ooh, a shy one." She places her hands under my chin and lifts my head. I refuse to meet her eyes. "You're in for a real treat tonight, Andy. Because I'm going to break the number one rule of magic. Do you know what the number one rule of magic is?"

"Never reveal the secret to a trick," I say, my voice low.

"That's right, never reveal the secret. But I'm going to make an exception for you. In fact, I'm going to tell you the secret to my trick before I even do it. Ready? The secret is…there is no secret!" Her voice grows faster and more animated. "I can just look at something and make it disappear! No misdirection, no sleight of hand."

"That's impossible."

"Remember when we talked about blind spots?" she asks. "It wasn't because I'm an optometry nerd; it was the setup for my trick." She takes a step back. "If I look at something and move my head so it sits in my blind spot," she turns her head slightly to the left, "it disappears from my sight, just like it would for you. And when I look back," she straightens her head, "it reappears. You with me?"

I nod.

She pulls an apple from her pocket.

"But, and this is a *big* but, Andy, if I shut my eye when the object is in my blind spot, and then look somewhere else, when I open my eye again, POOF! It disappears in real life."

"No way."

"Way. I mean, obviously only part of the object has to actually be in my blind spot for it to work. It's not like I can fit an entire car in there." She rolls her eyes. "I'm not sure how it works, but I know it's *what* I concentrate on that matters."

She jams the apple between my thighs. "Here, you try."

I stare at the apple. My eyes burn a hole in it. I don't just want to make it disappear. I want to smash her face with it, to make applesauce with her blood and snot.

She giggles.

"Can't do it, can you?"

"Tied up like this? No."

"Well, I'm not going to untie you. But I'll show you how it's done. Step one is taking this damn contact out." She pulls down her lower right eyelid, then pinches the lens. "That's better," she says. She blinks several times in rapid succession, then looks at me. "What do you think?"

The iris of her eye is tiger orange, with white stripes radiating outward from the center. Her pupil is blacker than any I've ever seen. I can't tell in this light, but I think it might be rotating, like a prop from a hypnosis trick.

"Is that real?" I ask. My mind drifts. "It's beautiful."

"You flatter me."

I can't stop staring at her eye. Yes, her pupil is definitely rotating.

Annie snaps her fingers in front of my face. "Pay attention, Andy. I need you to watch this, okay?" She gets on her knees in front of me and places her hands on my thighs, then looks up at me and bats her eyes. "Don't get any ideas. I know how guys like you think. I just want you to see me and the apple at the same time. No misdirection."

"Fine."

"Hush! I need to concentrate on the apple or it won't work right."

She stares at the apple. Her pupil spins faster. She takes a deep breath, then turns her head a bit to the left and shuts her right eye.

A breeze blows through the room. Is there a window open?

She counts to five under her breath, then looks up at me and opens her eye.

The apple disappears.

My jaw drops. "What the…"

"I bet you're trying to figure out how I did it, huh?" She beams. "I told you, it's not a trick. The apple's really gone."

I try to cover my shock with a joke. "You couldn't have set the apple on the table? Jesus, if your aim had been off just a little, you could've made my dick disappear!"

"Your dick was safe, Andy. I told you, I have to really concentrate on the object, and that's an image I don't want in my head." She shakes in disgust. "I don't know how it works—it is magic, after all—but I know how to control it."

"So has your eye always looked...like that?" I ask. I need to keep her talking.

"No." She walks to the mirror and pulls at her lower eyelid. "Ironically, it started after a botched Lasik operation at the mall where I found you. Electrical surge. Won enough in the lawsuit to buy this farm." She laughs. "There's a life lesson for you—don't trust your sight to a strip mall surgeon." She turns around and smiles. "Now, where were we?"

"Finish it," I say, desperately trying to buy a little more time.

"What do you mean, finish it?"

"Finish the trick. So you made the apple disappear. Big deal. That's the easy part. A real magician could bring it back."

"I never claimed to be a real magician. I said I could do magic. Big difference." She frowns. "And I *never* said anything about bringing it back."

"You said you'd let me go after you made me disappear. If you can't bring the apple back, how are you going to bring *me* back?"

"I never said I *couldn't* bring it back, either. But for this trick, *you're* going to bring the apple back."

"Is that what happened to Mancha?" My voice cracks. "Did you send your dog to fetch an apple and bring him back as a misshapen freak?" Mancha looks up at the mention of his name. "No offense, buddy."

She gasps.

"Don't be shocked, Annie. It wasn't hard to figure out. You made Mancha disappear, didn't you? And when you brought him back, he looked like, well..."

"Sort of," she whispers.

I nod. "I'm sorry, Annie. What happened?"

"I-I-I don't know. I told you, I have to really focus on something to make it disappear. But he started barking right as I was making some—" she catches herself "—some*thing* disappear and he broke my concentration." She wipes away a tear. "He reappeared a few hours later, like everything else does."

I freeze. "Everything else?"

"All the jars behind you? Those are some of the other things I made disappear."

I look in the mirror at the things floating in the jars. I can *almost* make out what they used to be, if I use my imagination.

"They're rodents, mostly," she says. "Mice, rats, squirrels. A few birds. They all came back wrong. And dead. Always dead." She looks down at Mancha. "I swear I didn't mean to make him disappear. It just happened. But he came back alive! I didn't know why at first, but eventually I figured it out. It's because he's smarter than those other animals. It has to be, right?"

I bite my tongue.

She walks over to Mancha's bed, squats down, and rubs his neck. "Sure, he looks awful now, but inside he's still the same sweet soul he's always been."

She looks up at me. I can see the anguish in her eyes. Well, in the left one at least. "But he can't tell me what happened to him!"

"And I can?"

"Yes! That's why I picked you, Andy. If anyone can understand my powers, it's you! I know you're not a real magician, but you understand how magic works."

"But I don't know anything about magical *powers*, Annie. My tricks are just tricks. There's no such thing as real magic." I pause. "At least, that's what I thought up until a few minutes ago."

I look at Mancha, then back at my captor. I smile. "I think maybe I can help you."

"Really? You'll help me?"

"I'll try." I almost have her now. "But you have to take the tape off me first."

She jumps up and backs away from Mancha. "Why would I do that?"

I keep my voice calm and level. "Think about it, Annie. What if there's something terrible over there and I have to defend myself? How can I do that if I'm duct taped to a chair?"

"That won't happen. There's nothing over there that can hurt you."

"How do you know that, Annie? Did Mancha tell you? Oh, that's right, Mancha can't tell you anything."

Her eyes widen.

"I'm sorry, Annie. That was mean. But you can see my point, can't you? I'll tell you what happened to Mancha. I promise. But first you have to cut this tape."

"No, no, no, no, no!" Annie paces back and forth. "You're just trying to trick me! If I cut you loose, you'll just run away. You won't help me. Someone like you would *never* help someone like me on his own."

I feel the situation slipping out of control. "Someone like me?"

"Yes, someone like you," she snaps. Her eye is glowing now. "Someone who thinks they're better than everyone else. Someone who wouldn't give a woman like me the time of day if you weren't taped to a chair in my basement."

"That's not true, Annie." I nervously lick my lips and try not to stare at her eye.

"Of course it's true!" she cries. "You didn't even remember that I asked for your autograph last night! I was the only person who did, AND YOU DIDN'T REMEMBER ME!"

"You're right, I didn't remember you. Not at first." My mind is racing, searching for the right words. "But come on, I just woke up. I didn't know where I was or what happened to me. Plus, I have this nasty bump on my head. I was lucky I remembered my own name. But I remember you now."

"You do?"

"Of course I do. You were there. You liked all my tricks. You even laughed at my lame jokes. And when the show ended, you came up and got my autograph. I remember." I sigh. I'm back in control.

"What was I wearing?"

Shit.

"I'm sorry, what?"

"I asked, what was I wearing? If you remember all that stuff about me, surely you remember what I was wearing, don't you?"

"Uhm…"

"How about where I was sitting? Do you remember that? Was I with anyone else, or was I there by myself? Do you remember any of that, or are you just lying to me so I'll let you go?"

"Annie, please, calm down and we can—"

"I WILL NOT CALM DOWN!" She kicks the folding chair across the room. "YOU don't get to tell me to do ANYTHING! You got that?"

Mancha's mouths bark in unison, a discordant sound that makes me wince.

"Jesus, what was I thinking? Why did I ever think you would help me? I'm such an idiot!" She pulls at her hair. "Shut up, Mancha!" she screams. "Mommy can't concentrate!"

Mancha whimpers and crawls into the corner.

She marches toward me and pokes my chest. "Listen to me, Andy. You're going to help—"

"Fuck off!" I shout. "I'm not helping you do anything!"

She grabs me by the throat and pushes my head back. "Yes, you are. Whether you want to or not. You, of all people, should appreciate my gift, and what I can do with it. I'm special! Don't you get it?" She lets go of me and takes a step back. She looks at the piles of clothes in the corner. "No, you're just like all the others."

Others?

"You could come back totally fine, you know. You're smart. The smartest one yet. If you didn't have such a shitty attitude, you probably *would* come back fine. But no, you have to be such a baby about it." She rubs her eyes like she's crying. "*Oh, Annie, please don't hurt me,*" she cries. "*Annie, please don't make me disappear. Wah wah wah!*" She snorts.

"Well, I'll tell you the same thing I told the others—if something bad happens to you, it's YOUR fault! Not mine! If you come back with eyes on your chest or a cock on your forehead, it's YOUR fault!"

I spit in her face.

She slaps me. "You shouldn't have done that," she says as she wipes the saliva from her cheek.

"Fuck you, Annie."

"Fuck me? Funny, it looks like *you're* the one who's about to be fucked, Andy."

She pushes my head back again until my neck pops. Her pupil is rotating so fast now, it's as if I'm looking into a tornado. "Am I still in your blind spot, Andy? Because you're about to be in mine." Her grip tightens. "I'm going to make you disappear now. And don't worry about the apple. It'll show up by itself in a few hours. You just pay attention so you can tell me what it's like over there when you come back. I need to know what happens to the things I make disappear. Do you think you can do that?" She lets go of my neck. My head snaps forward. "Well?"

I squeeze my eyes shut and shake my head, trying not to cry.

"You can shut your eyes all you want, Andy. It won't make a difference. I can still see you."

"Mancha, say goodbye to Andy!" Mancha's mouths yip in unison.

I open my eyes and look up at her. "Annie, please, you don't have to do this!" I'm sobbing now.

She kisses me on the forehead, then leans back, turns her head, and closes her eye. Orange light threatens to burn through her eyelid.

An icy wind whips through the room, blowing the newspaper clippings in a circle around near the ceiling. The cabinet behind me shakes. Jars rattle against each other. One falls to the ground and shatters. The smell of formaldehyde fills my nostrils as the room around me grows dark.

"Trust me, Andy, it's for the best."

I scream.

Annie's voice whispers out of the darkness.

"You'll see."

THE WORLD ENDS AT THE
WORLD'S END

Once upon a time, there was a little old woman and a little old man who lived in a little old cottage near a lazy old river. One afternoon, the little old woman baked a gingerbread man. She gave him raisins for eyes, a cinnamon drop for a mouth, and chocolate chips for buttons. Then she put him in the oven to bake.

When she opened the oven door, the gingerbread man jumped out and ran through the kitchen and out of the cottage. "Please don't eat me!" he shouted. "For the stars are finally right and it is time for the sleeping city of R'lyeh to rise and great Cthulhu to awaken. *Ph'nglui mglw'nafh Cthulhu R'lyeh wgah'nagl fhtagn!*"

He continued to run, from the cottage into town and then into the forest beyond, all the while singing to anyone who tried to catch him, "Run, run as fast as you can, you can't catch me, *Cthulhu fhtagn!*"

So caught up was he in mocking those chasing him that he failed to see a tree had fallen across the trail. Nor did he see the dwarf whose beard was stuck in a crack in the tree. Quick as a wink, the dwarf flipped the gingerbread man into the air, snapped his jaws shut, and bit the gingerbread man's head clean off.

And that was the end of the gingerbread man.

***

Snow-White and Rose-Red were walking through the woods collecting sticks for the family's wood pile when they came upon an enormous tree which had fallen across the trail. The scent of ginger and cinnamon drew the girls closer. Sitting next to the tree was a dwarf with a shriveled-up face and white beard, eating the last bits of a gingerbread man. His long beard, which was stuck in a gash in the tree, was covered in crumbs. He hummed to himself as he picked at his beard and licked his fingers. When his beard was clean, he looked up and saw the girls watching him in silence.

"Why are you just standing there, mouths agape?!" He shook his fists. "Can't you see I'm trapped? This tree has captured my beautiful white beard and I cannot get loose. Set me free this instant!"

Despite the dwarf's belligerence, the sisters tried to think of a way to free him. After a few minutes, Rose-Red told the dwarf she would run and get someone else.

"Idiot!" cried the dwarf. "There are already two of you here now. Why would you leave to get more people? Can't you think of something better?"

Snow-White thought for a second longer. She grabbed a pair of scissors from her bag, and before the dwarf could object, she cut his beard and set him free.

"Stupid cows!" He stomped his feet and flailed his arms about. "To cut off a piece of my beard, of which I am so proud! You'll both pay for this. Mark my words, you will pay!"

A great growl silenced the dwarf as a large black bear ambled onto the path. "Pay for what?" the bear demanded.

The dwarf fell to his knees. "Please do not eat me, Mr. Bear! My beautiful beard was trapped in this tree, and rather than return to town to fetch help as I so humbly suggested, these two horrible creatures cut my beard. They have made a laughingstock of me, and must be punished. I beg you, please eat them instead, for I am very old and my meat is no doubt tough and stringy and sure to induce gastrointestinal distress, but they are young and soft and fresh and—"

"Enough!" The bear stood on its hind legs and glared down at the dwarf. The dwarf shrunk into himself, while Snow-White and Rose-Red froze in place. "Nobody will be eaten today," said the bear. "But the time of unmasking is at hand!"

With a single swipe of his giant paw, the bear peeled the dwarf's skin from his face. The dwarf's eyes shone impossibly white and impossibly wide against the glistening red meat.

Rose-Red and Snow-White screamed.

"Do not fear, my dears," said the bear. "It is I, your friend Mr. Bear, who let you play on his back on cold winter nights while I slept in front of the fire."

Snow-White, standing closest to the dwarf, curtsied. "Forgive us, Mr. Bear, for we did not recognize you. How has your spring—"

Mr. Bear ripped off her face before she could finish. "Have you found the Yellow Sign?" He laughed, a high warbling sound that chilled

Rose-Red's blood anew. "And now, sweet Rose-Red, it is your turn to meet the king." He swiped at her cheek, but Rose-Red was too fast. She ducked underneath his outstretched paw and ran into the forest. As she fled deeper into the woods, she heard Mr. Bear bellow, "No matter! I will unmask myself!" The hellish sounds of ripping flesh and maniacal laughter followed Rose-Red as the forest swallowed her whole.

***

Isabelle was hopelessly lost. Three days earlier, as punishment for letting slip a comment about the evil queen and a pair of red-hot iron slippers, her stepmother had given her a sieve and a simple command: "Go, fill it at the Well of the World's End, and bring it back to me full, or woe betide you."

She'd cried the first night when her father had not come looking for her. There were tears again on the second night, but these were tears of anger over the mistreatment she'd suffered at the hands of her stepmother. This morning she'd awoken determined to fill the sieve out of spite more than obligation or duty.

Near mid-morning, she met an old woman and an old man wandering through the woods, searching for a gingerbread man.

"Have you heard of the Well of the World's End?" she asked them.

"The Well at the World's End?" The old man nodded. "It's back that way." He pointed in the direction from which they'd come.

"No, I think it's the other way." The old woman pointed in the opposite direction.

"Thank you both," said Isabelle, "but I'm looking for the Well *of* the World's End, not the Well *at* the World's End."

"Well, that's a different well altogether," said the old man.

"So, do you know where it is?"

"Sorry, never heard of it," he said.

Isabelle sighed and turned away.

"Wait!" The old woman's face lit up. "I think I remember our gingerbread man saying something about it. At first he was jabbering on about the stars finally being right, and how it was time for the sleeping city of R'lyeh to rise and great Cthulhu to awaken. Does that make any sense to you?"

"I'm afraid not," said Isabelle. "You said he mentioned the well?"

"Right, right. Later he said something about a well on the shores of the Lake of Hali, near dim, lost Carcosa maybe?" She rubbed her chin. "Then again, he said a lot of crazy things, even for a talking cookie."

Isabelle thanked them and took her leave. She walked for perhaps another hour when she came upon a dark-haired girl dressed in red sitting on a log, crying.

"Whatever is the matter?" Isabelle asked as she handed the girl her handkerchief.

In between sobs, the girl, who said her name was Rose-Red, shared an implausible story about a terribly rude dwarf with a white beard and her sister and a horrific bear who'd brutally killed them both before peeling off its own face.

Isabelle could hardly believe Rose-Red's tale. Something terrible had obviously happened—how else to explain the blood splattered on her face, hair, and clothing—but a bear that peeled off its own face?

"My poor sweet sister Snow-White is dead!" Rose-Red buried her face in her hands. She blew her nose with such force that her hair blew back. When she finished, she offered the kerchief back to the girl.

"No, you can keep it," Isabelle said. "Wait, your sister is Snow White? *The* Snow White? Seven dwarves, evil queen, poison apple?"

"No, not *that* Snow White." Rose-Red shook her head. "My sister is"—she sniffled—"*was* Snow-White, with a hyphen. But that *other* Snow White bites one poison apple and overnight, she's the famous one."

A low, malevolent growl echoed through the woods, and a hideous creature with a glistening red face and evil grin shambled onto the path. "There you are, Rose-Red!" The bear's voice was deep and gravelly, as if its mouth were packed with graveyard dirt. "Have you found the Yellow Sign yet?"

Rose-Red shoved Isabelle toward the woods behind them. "Run!" Isabelle tried to drag Rose-Red with her, but she refused. "My sister is dead," she said, "and so too am I." She walked toward the bear, who stood on its back feet, towering over her.

Isabelle sprinted into the forest. Behind her, Rose-Red let out a single bloodcurdling scream. The woods went silent.

***

Isabelle ran until her lungs burned and her legs could carry her no farther. She needed to rest, so she hid behind a tree where she could still see the trail.

Some time passed, and she thought it might be safe to leave when she heard something walking along the path toward her. She crouched and readied herself to flee if it was the bear.

A smallish man came into view. He had a narrow head, flattened nose, and wide, bulgy eyes. He sang to himself in a language she did not recognize. *"Ph'nglui mglw'nafh Cthulhu R'lyeh wgah'nagl fhtagn!"* Over and over he sang the words, sending a chill down her spine. But she needed help, and he was the first person she'd seen since Rose-Red, so she left her hiding place.

"Please, sir, can you help me?" she asked.

The man started, but quickly composed himself. "Of course, my lady, I will help if I can. But when we have finished, I ask that you return the favor, for I also find myself in need of assistance."

She agreed, then told him about her stepmother and the sieve and her fruitless search for the Well of the World's End, not the Well *at* the World's End, thank you very much, because that's a completely different well altogether. Had he heard of it?

"Heard of it?" He grinned. "Near the Lake of Hali?"

"And dim, lost Carcosa?" Could the old woman's talking cookie have been telling the truth?

"The very same. As luck would have it, I'm headed to a masquerade ball at the palace, and my route will take me very near the well."

"Will you show me where?" she asked.

He bowed. "It would be my pleasure."

Isabelle could not believe her good fortune! Of course, there was still the matter of his small request. What would he ask for in return? A kiss? Her hand in marriage? While she'd heard tales of frogs who turned into princes with a simple kiss, she wasn't sure what would happen if she kissed a man who merely *looked* like a frog.

"The Lake of Hali is still a day's walk from here," he told her, "and these woods are not safe after dark. I think we should walk a bit longer and then make camp for the night."

She agreed, and before long, they found a suitable space and settled in. Over a meal of dried fish and a paste that smelled worse than it tasted, he regaled her with tales of his adventures, and the guild to which he belonged, the Esoteric Order of Dagon, or Erotic Odor of Dragon, or something like that. To be honest, she'd only been half-listening, as she was keeping an ear out for the bear. Should she warn her new traveling companion of the unholy ursid? Not wanting to scare him off, she kept quiet for a while longer.

That night, she dreamt of an impossible city on the shores of a black lake. It sat under a great blackness lit by black stars, ruled by an ancient entity wearing tattered yellow robes.

She awoke early, hungry and unrested. After a quick breakfast of more dried fish, they set off. Toward evening, she finally spotted the cyclopean towers of Carcosa, reaching skyward at unnatural angles. It was the city from her dream! And were there *two* suns sinking behind the Lake of Hali? Surely, her tired eyes were playing tricks on her.

"Beautiful, is it not?" her companion asked.

"I don't know if that's the word I'd use."

"It's in the eye of the beholder." He pointed toward a side trail. "The well is this way. Follow me."

At the end of the trail waited the Well of the World's End. She lowered her sieve into the well, but it would not hold water. She tried again and again, but always met the same result.

"I can tell you how to fill it," the man said, "but you must remember your promise to help me when we are finished."

"Of course."

He showed her how to plug the holes with moss and clay. She lowered the sieve once again into the well. This time the water did not run out! She'd be able to bring a full bucket back to her stepmother, which she planned to pour over the wicked woman's head.

"Thank you, kind sir. Now I can fulfill my stepmother's request." He bowed. "But first, what would you have me do in return?" She lowered her eyes. "Perhaps a kiss?"

"No."

"Would you ask for my hand?"

"Heavens, no!"

"Then what? A quick coupling on the beach, under these alien stars?"

"Would you?"

"Heavens, no!"

"Just checking," he sighed. "Actually, I need you to chop off my head."

Isabelle gasped. "What? Why would you ask such a thing of me? I won't do it. I *can't* do it."

"I'm sorry," he said. "But while Captain Marsh was quite clear on the 'what,' unfortunately he was a bit hazy on the 'why.' Nevertheless, as a disciple of the Order, I am sworn to obey, and so I must insist you fulfill your end of our agreement and remove my head."

"Or, perhaps, you will unmask instead," said Mr. Bear, who had snuck up when they were patching the sieve.

"Indeed?" asked the man.

"Indeed." Mr. Bear lifted his paw, claws extended.

"I wear no mask," said the man.

"No mask? No mask!" The bear grabbed the strange man's head between his massive paws and ripped it from his body. And lo! and behold, there now towered over them the great dreamer Cthulhu, master of R'lyeh. The bear fell to his knees, blubbering, and Isabelle raced screaming into the Lake of Hali, where she was consumed by the yellow misshapen things frothing in the waves.

And nobody lived happily ever after.

In fact, nobody lived at all.

NICHOLAS

Magic is real, you know? And that means it's gonna die someday. Even the sun's gonna die eventually. You think magic's more powerful than that? Keep dreaming.

Of course, good old Nicholas thought the magic would last forever. He'd lived on it for centuries, after all. Lived on it too well, in fact, to the point that we had to totally retrofit the sleigh. Added seatbelt extenders, doubled the width of the bench seat, thickened the cushions with eight-inch memory foam, and totally beefed up the suspension. We filmed the whole thing for that year's office party; called it "Plump My Ride." Big guy got a real kick out of it too.

That was back when he was still jolly, of course.

He called it a "symbiotic relationship." He gave the kids presents, and they gave him their hearts. In retrospect, it was more parasitic. Because guess what? The kids today don't believe in him anymore. Not enough, anyway. The world out there's gone to hell—pornography, violence, little baby beauty pageants... And the Internet's pumping it straight into their empty little skulls, a 24/7 supercharged Technicolor temporal injection chronicling man's inhumanity to man and just about everything else on the fucking planet. Bottom line, kids just grow up too fast these days. Time was, they'd believe in Nick for 10, maybe 12 years. He's lucky if he gets five now.

So the magic's fading. And without it, Nicholas is starving.

One day a few weeks ago he was taking a group of investors on a tour of the factory floor when his pants fell down around his ankles. He tried to laugh it off and promised to double up on the milk and cookies, but nobody was buying it. Especially not the sharks, who left without giving him a single cent.

The next night, a huge storm blew in, and Nicholas said he was going out to check on the sleigh. That was the last anyone saw of jolly Saint Nick.

What came back from that blizzard was anything but merry. Gone were the broad face and little round belly we'd known for centuries; in their place, a skeletal mask and excess rolls of shiny, sallow skin hanging from his neck, chest, and stomach. His twinkling eyes had disappeared, replaced by icy, black marbles. His snow-white beard was matted thick with clotted blood, a perfect frame for his sharp, crimson teeth.

He devoured everything in the facility. Milk. Cookies. Even the hydroponic carrots we grew special for Rudolph. Killed all the reindeer too, starting with his red-nosed favorite. Sucked the marrow straight from their bones, he did.

And then he turned on us.

There were over 400 of us on the floor that day. There's only five of us left now. We've been barricaded in the office for nearly a week. The little food we had ran out two days ago. Water's almost gone. Hermey went out to look for Mrs. Claus last night. We haven't heard from him since.

We're hungry.

Nicholas is hungrier.

Wait, what was that clatter? Is that someone on the roof?

CATERWAUL

One warm, windy Wednesday morning, Marlin Hambush opened the front door to find a dead cat on his porch.

This was troubling for two reasons: one, it was Wednesday, which Marlin considered the least likely day on which to find a dead cat on one's porch. Two, the cat in question wasn't just dead; it was also missing its head.

This was not good. Not good at all.

He was already late for work. And to make matters worse, Marlin had recently had a bit of a tiff with his neighbors over the very feline that now rested—sans noggin—at his feet.

When Marvin first moved in, they'd fought over the cat's habit of leaving dead animals on his porch. As disgusting as he found the habit to be, he now accepted them as gestures of the cat's goodwill; the feline equivalent of saying, "Look, I know my owners are horrible people, so here, have a dead bird. I pulled its eyes out for you."

The most recent fight concerned the cat's propensity for half-burying its shit in his wife's garden.

This morning, though, it appeared someone had taken it upon themselves to plant the pooper in question upon his front porch.

Marlin considered his options. Obviously, he couldn't just leave it there. His wife might step in it. Marlin Jr. might want to play with it. And what would happen if the neighbors walked over and saw what was left of their precious fur baby splayed across Marlin's welcome mat? Certainly they wouldn't think *he* did it, would they? Even people as awful as they were would recognize it made no sense for him to leave their dead cat on his own porch. If he'd planned on making such a blatantly bold and bloody declaration of war, wouldn't he leave it on *their* porch? Marlin hadn't read *The Art of War*, but he imagined there had to be an entry on the stupidity of attacking yourself with the dead cat of your enemy.

So Marlin grabbed a rag, picked up the cat, and tossed it into the dumpster in the alley. On his way back, he stopped and snatched the dead cat's collar from around his garden gnome's neck.

"I'll deal with you later," he said to the gnome. He took the collar into the garage and threw it in a shoebox full of bloodstained collars.

**

Later that evening, Marlin went out to the garage and opened the box. The number of collars had grown considerably over the past six months. Mostly cats, but also a few he thought might come from those little yippie dogs so many young women seemed to carry around as fashion accessories these days.

"What's the matter, Marlin? Cat got your tongue?" his garden gnome asked, leaning against the doorway to the back yard.

"Shut up, Gnick," Marlin said, making a point to pronounce the gnome's name "Guh-Nick."

"No, *you* shut up, Marlin." Gnick hopped on a footstool, then climbed up onto a cooler. "If you're going to talk to me, at least have the decency to say my name correctly. It's pronounced Nick. The 'G' is silent."

"Whatever. Why'd you do it?"

"Do what?"

"You know."

"I know lots of things, Marlin." Gnick tamped tobacco into his pipe. "Except whatever it is you're talking about right now."

"Fine. That's how you want to play?" Marlin put the lid back on the box of collars and sat down across from Gnick. "Why'd you kill my neighbor's cat?"

"I think the question should be: Why do you care so much about this particular cat, Marlin?"

"Because you left this one on my porch," Marlin said. "I don't know what you did with the other ones. And I don't care. But you left this one on my porch."

"Look, Marlin, this is a quiet street."

"And...?"

"And I'm just doing my part to make sure it stays that way. When those cats start fighting or fucking or whatever else they do when the sun goes down, it makes me crazy! I can't take the constant caterwauling! I hate it!" Gnick stood up on the cooler. "This is *my* neighborhood, Marlin.

My house, my yard, my garden… It was mine long before you got here, and it'll be mine long after you're gone."

"But *I* own the house. My name is on the mortgage. So technically, I own you too."

"That sounds good on paper, Marlin, but we both know *I* really own this place. And anyone who lives in it." Gnick wiggled his fingers at Marlin. "When you moved in, you moved under my spell."

"That doesn't even make sense."

"The point is, when something—or someone—makes too much noise around my house, I'll put a stop to it."

Gnick took a deep breath and closed his eyes for a moment. "That aside, do you know what I hate even more than caterwauling, Marlin?"

"Doggerwauling?"

Gnick's eyes popped open. "What?"

"Doggerwauling. It's like caterwauling, except with dogs—"

"You think it's funny, Marlin?" Gnick jumped onto Marlin's lap and poked him in the chest. "You think it's funny that my ears are seventy-five times more sensitive than yours? Does it amuse you that I hear things you can't, like whose name your wife whispered when you used to have relations? Never mind," he said, before Marlin had a chance to answer. "That was a low blow. She only whispers your name, stud." He climbed back down onto the cooler.

"I thought you said fifty."

"What?"

"The last time you complained about your ears, you said they were fifty times more sensitive than mine. This time you said seventy-five."

"Fifty, seventy-five, whatever, Marlin. I'm a gnome, not a mathematician."

"Sorry. So, what is it?"

"What's what?"

"What is it that you hate more than caterwauling?"

"Besides stupid questions?"

"Yes."

"Getting shit on, Marlin. Call me crazy, but I hate getting shit on. And that cat tried to take a dump on my foot last night."

"He's been doing that in the wife's petunias a lot lately too."

"I know. But just like every other time something needs done around here, I'm the only one with balls enough to fix it."

"That's great, Gnick," Marlin said. "But what if the neighbors saw it? I'd be in a complete world of shit, instead of just a flower garden full of it."

Gnick shrugged.

Marlin sighed. He knew arguing with Gnick was as pointless as trying to get rid of him, but sometimes he couldn't help it. Despite being cursed with a killer garden gnome, Marlin loved his house. He had since the day they first saw it. And there was no way he was going to move out, no matter how hard Gnick made it to stay.

He got up to leave. "I have to go in now, Gnick. Marlin Jr. has a cold." At the door, he turned back toward the gnome. "Please don't leave any more cats on my porch."

The sound of Marlin Jr.'s coughing echoed over the back yard. "That sounds like a real nasty cough there, Marlin," said Gnick. "I sure hope your boy feels better soon."

Marlin turned off the light and went inside.

***

Marlin Jr. did not feel better that night. Nor did he feel better the next several nights, despite visits to two different doctors and an urgent care facility. The nurse at the urgent care told them the flu was going around town, and cough syrup, ibuprofen, and rest was the only thing they could do.

The flu was going around Marlin's plant too. They were so short-staffed Marlin's boss told him he'd have to pull a double shift.

Marlin protested. He told his boss about how sick Marlin Jr. was. But his boss didn't care. "Those widgets ain't gonna widget themselves," he said over his shoulder as he walked away. Marlin called his wife, let her yell at him a bit, and went back to work.

***

The next week was a blur. Marlin pulled a double shift every other day. Marlin Jr. coughed and cried every day and night. And Gnick sported a new collar nearly every morning. Marlin had no idea there were so many cats in the neighborhood. He hadn't heard a single one the past few nights. Of course, thanks to the double shifts and some sleeping pills, he hadn't heard much of anything. Even Marlin Jr.'s coughing fits seemed like a distant memory.

Until this morning.

***

"What do you mean, he's gone?" Marlin asked his wife, rubbing sleep from his eyes.

"I mean he's gone! He's not in the house! He's not in the yard! He's not anywhere!"

She meant Marlin Jr. He'd been coughing when Marlin had got home the night before, as usual. And Marlin had taken a sleeping pill and gone to bed, as usual. What wasn't usual, however, was his wife waking him up, hysterical, screaming that Marlin Jr. was gone.

Marlin got out of bed, threw on some pants, and together they searched the house, the yard, and the garage. Then they called 911.

***

Marlin had never been inside an interrogation room before, but he'd seen enough of them on TV over the years to know someone was watching from the other side of the mirror. What he didn't know was why the police seemed more interested in his box of collars than his missing son.

"Let me get this straight," Marlin said to the two detectives sitting across from him. "My son's missing and you want to talk about a box of cat collars? Why aren't you out looking for him instead of wasting time with this?"

"Patrols are looking for him," said the first detective, a tall, skinny blond man Marlin decided was the Starsky of the two. "And the sooner we get this out of the way, the sooner we can all get back out there and help."

Marlin leaned back in his chair and sighed. "Fine. What would you like to know?"

The second officer, who by default became Hutch, despite being chubby and bald, asked Marlin about the bloody fingerprints they found on the collars and the box.

"They're mine," Marlin said. "It's not my blood though. It's not even human. It's cat. Maybe a little dog. Just check the DNA like they do on TV. You'll see."

Starsky looked up from his yellow legal notepad. "Cat blood? You get off on killing cats, Marlin? Got some unresolved pussy issues?" His partner stifled a laugh.

"What about dogs? Unconditional love not enough for someone like you?" asked Hutch.

"No! I mean, yes, unconditional love is more than enough for someone like me."

"Then why kill them?" Starsky set down his pen. "You have to get *something* out of it."

"This is ridiculous! I didn't kill them." Marlin couldn't believe the questions they were asking. He'd been "Employee of the Month" three times in the past year alone. And while three-time "Employees of the Month" were a lot of things (loyal, hardworking, and dependable sprang to mind), they were definitely *not* psycho cat killers.

Unfortunately for Gnick, three-time "Employees of the Month" were also honest.

Marlin took a deep breath. "It was Gnick," he said in a low voice. "Gnick killed the cats."

"Guh-nick? How do you spell that?"

"G-N-I-C-K. It's actually pronounced Nick," said Marlin. "The G is supposed to be silent. I call him Guh-nick because—never mind, it's not important right now. The important thing is finding Marlin Jr., which is why I don't understand your fascination with Gnick's box of dead cat collars."

"Did he just say the cat collars were dead?" Starsky asked Hutch.

"No, I think he meant the collars belonged to dead cats," Hutch said.

"Cats that a Mister..." Starsky checked his notes. "...G-N-I-C-K, pronounced Nick with a silent 'G,' killed. That sound about right, Marlin?"

"Yes."

"And who is this Gnick?" Hutch asked.

"Our garden gnome."

Starsky set his pen down. "Your garden gnome killed the cats?"

"No."

"But you just said he did."

"I mean yes, he killed them, but no, he's not *my* garden gnome. He just came with the house. I tried throwing him away at first, but he was always right back in the garden the next morning. I used to think the neighbors were playing a trick on me."

"Used to?"

"Yeah, until I found out Gnick was just walking back on his own every night."

"Your garden gnome can walk?" asked Hutch.

"That's not all he can do. He can walk, talk—"

Starsky snickered. "Can he chew bubble gum at the same time?"

Marlin cocked his head. "At the same time he's talking? How would I know?"

"Not when he's talking, Marlin. That would be rude. Can he walk and chew bubble gum at the same time?" Starsky asked.

"Why does that matter?"

"Because that would make him a pretty special gnome, Marlin."

"That's not the type of gnome you'd want to just throw away," said Hutch.

"He's not special! He's an albatross!"

"An albatross?" Starsky picked up his pen. "I thought he was a gnome?"

The speaker above the mirror clicked on. *"It's a figure of speech, guys. I think Marlin means Gnick is the albatross that hangs around his neck."*

"Exactly!" Marlin pointed his finger at the speaker. "She gets it. I can't get rid of him, no matter how hard I try. That stupid gnome is a curse. A mean, nasty, cat-killing curse."

Hutch reached into an evidence box sitting on the floor and pulled out a large plastic bag. Gnick was inside the bag. "You mean this garden gnome? He doesn't look that cursed to me." Inside the bag, Gnick put his forefinger over his lips and winked at Marlin.

Marlin blanched, then nodded at the officers.

"You wanna explain all the red around his mouth?" Starsky asked. "Did you put lipstick on your gnome?" He turned to Hutch and pursed his lips. "I think maybe Marlin here has a thing for Gnick."

Hutch laughed. "You may be on to something. Sure doesn't look like a g-normal g-nome to me."

"That's cat blood too," Marlin said.

"Of course it is. Say, Marlin, do you happen to know *why* Gnick killed all these cats?"

"He said he couldn't stand their caterwauling." Marlin rubbed his temples. "According to Gnick, a gnome's ears are fifty to seventy-five times more sensitive than ours."

"Fifty to seventy-five?" Hutch whistled. "That's a pretty wide range, Marlin."

"He's a garden gnome, not a mathematician."

"Duly noted."

"So if I heard cats making a ruckus at night, I knew I'd find a collar around Gnick's neck the next day, like a little trophy. I don't know why I kept them. I just did."

"What can you tell us about this?" Hutch pulled another bag out of the box, then slid it across the table to Marlin. In it was a binky, splattered with red. "Is that cat's blood too?"

Marlin's blood froze. "That's Marlin Jr.'s binky. Where did you find it?"

"It was in the box of collars. Another of Gnick's trophies?"

Marlin lunged across the table and grabbed at the bag. "What did you do to Marlin Jr.? Answer me!"

Starsky snatched Gnick back out of Marlin's reach, while Hutch ran around the table, grabbed Marlin by the shoulders, and pushed him back down into his seat.

Inside the plastic bag, Gnick flipped Marlin the bird.

"Did you see that?" Marlin shouted. "He stuck his middle finger up at me!"

"I didn't see anything," Starsky said, "except a grown man trying to attack a garden gnome in a police evidence bag."

Hutch slapped Marlin on the back of the head. "You can't touch the evidence, Marlin! Don't you watch TV?"

"I'm sorry," Marlin said. "But Gnick did something to Marlin Jr. I *know* he did."

"How do you know that?" Hutch asked as he returned to his seat.

"Because Marlin Jr.'s had a cold the past couple weeks. He's been up coughing every night, and I'm sure the noise was bothering Gnick. I just didn't think he'd do anything to my little boy."

"Why would you think that?"

"Because Gnick's a dick, but he's not a murderer. At least I didn't think he was."

Hutch looked at Gnick, then at Marlin. "You know what I think, Marlin?"

"No."

"I think *you* think we're a couple of yahoos you can fool with some story about being cursed with a killer garden gnome."

Starsky snorted. "I'm insulted, Marlin. A killer gnome? That's the best you got?"

"It's not a story!"

"You're right, it's not." Hutch slammed the table with both hands. "It's a friggin' cliché!"

Marlin slunk back into his seat. "W-w-what?"

Starsky sighed. "A killer garden gnome is one of the oldest tropes around, Marlin. You're certainly not the first person to use it."

"Yeah, why not try something a bit more original?" Hutch asked.

"Well, the cursed part at least showed a little imagination," said Starsky.

"Seriously?" Hutch waved his hands in the air and imitated Marlin's voice. *"Ooh, a killer gnome haunts my garden. I tried throwing him away, but he just keeps coming back. Ooh, he must be cursed!"*

"Well, when you put it that way, it does seem pretty lame," Starsky said.

Marlin frowned. The detectives' new tack confused him. "What are you talking about?"

"I'm talking about of all the ideas you could've tried, you picked one of the lamest ones out there," said Hutch. "Why not tell us Black Annis broke in to your house and ate Marlin Jr.?"

Marlin made a face. "Black anus?"

"*Annis*, Marlin. Black *Annis*. She was a bogeyman-type creature in English folklore with iron claws and a taste for the succulent flesh of young children."

"Mind you, we wouldn't have believed that either," said Starsky, "but at least it would have showed a little more imagination on your part."

"But it's the truth! Gnick took Marlin Jr.!"

"It's not the truth, Marlin. It's lazy." Hutch pointed his finger at Marlin to punctuate his point. "If I came across this story in a book, I'd hunt down the author and kick him in the nuts for being such a lazy hack. But since he's not here, I guess yours will have to do." He walked around the table and gestured for Marlin to rise. "Come on, stand up."

"I will not!"

Starsky grabbed Marlin under the armpits and lifted him out of his seat.

"You can't do this!" Marlin turned his head toward the mirror. "Tell them they can't do this!"

The speaker on the wall above the mirror crackled to life.

"Nah, it's okay, guys. Go ahead and kick him in the nuts."

The speaker switched back off.

Hutch swung his leg back, while Marlin tried to cross his to soften the blow.

"Stop!"

Hutch's foot stopped mid-kick. He looked up at the speaker. "Was that you, Chief?"

"No."

"Then who was it?" Starsky looked around.

A ripping sound filled the room as Gnick tore his way out of the evidence bag. "It was me, you stupid fucknuts! Haven't you been listening?" He jumped across the table and snatched out both of Hutch's eyes. "So I'm a cliché, am I?" He lowered his head and rammed Starsky in

132

the stomach. "I'm lazy, huh? Could a lazy cliché do this?" He punched his clay fist through Starsky's abdomen and ripped out a handful of ropy intestines. Blood and shit and half-digested donuts spilled out onto the interrogation room floor. Hutch, blinded from Gnick's attack, slipped in the pool of viscera and cracked his head on the concrete floor.

"Marlin! Let's go!" Gnick shouted as he ran toward the door.

Marlin looked at Gnick. He looked at Starsky's guts strewn all over the floor. He looked at Hutch lying in Starsky's guts. He looked for Hutch's eyes, but didn't see them. Did Gnick eat them?

Marlin fainted. When he came to, Hutch was standing over him, snapping his fingers in front of his face.

"Earth to Marlin. You in there, buddy?"

"I'm sorry, I, I... Did I pass out?"

"Yeah." He helped Marlin back up to his seat. "You were smiling though. What were you thinking about?"

Marlin looked at Gnick, still in the evidence bag. Hutch still had both of his eyes. And Starsky's guts were still contained to his abdominal cavity.

"Nothing," he whispered.

"Marlin, did you just dream that Gnick came to life, killed both of us, and rescued you?" Starsky asked.

Hutch cocked his head and grinned. "You did, didn't you?"

"No."

"Marlin, Marlin, Marlin... What are we going to do with you?" Starsky checked his notes. "What did you say you do for a living?"

"I work in the widget factory."

"Thank God you're not a writer, because that rescue fantasy would be strike two. And you know what happens at strike three?"

"You kick me in the nuts again?"

"Again?" Starsky laughed. "Were you just fantasizing about me kicking you in the nuts?"

"I wasn't fantasizing about it."

"Yes, you were. You fantasized about me kicking you in the nuts and then Gnick here came to life and killed us, didn't he?"

"How'd he do it?" Hutch asked. "Bash my brains in? Rip my arms off? Burst through my chest?"

Marlin pointed to Hutch. "He poked your eyes out like the Three Stooges." He looked at Starsky. "And he pulled your guts out. And then you," he pointed back to Hutch, "slipped in his guts and cracked your skull open on the floor."

"He did, did he?" Starsky asked. "Did he say, 'Nyuck nyuck nyuck' too?"

"Or maybe it was more 'g-nyuck g-nyuck g-nyuck'?" Hutch laughed.

"Good one," said Starsky. He picked up his legal pad and flipped back to the first page. "Let's recap, Marlin. So far you've given us a killer gnome story—"

"—a *cursed* killer gnome," Hutch added.

"Right, a cursed killer gnome to explain your missing son, and a fantasy escape sequence when you realized we weren't buying it. Wanna try one more time?"

"I know it sounds crazy, but Gnick really did kill all those cats."

The speaker crackled back to life. *"And a couple dogs. Don't you dare forget about those sweet, innocent doggos!"*

Marlin sighed. "And a couple dogs. And I don't know why I kept the collars. I'm sure it made sense at the time, but like I said, I've been under a lot of stress lately—"

"From the double shifts and Marlin Jr.'s cold?" Hutch interrupted.

"Yes."

"What about the bedroom?" Starsky asked.

"The bedroom?"

"You know, marital relations. Any problems there?"

Marlin's cheeks flushed. "That's none of your business!"

"Marlin, your son is missing and you want us to believe your garden gnome may have killed him." Starsky set his legal pad on the table, then gave Marlin a cold stare. "Right now, *everything* is our business."

Marlin swallowed. "Okay, yes. Rose has been a bit distant lately."

"You sure about that?"

"Yeah, maybe Rose isn't the problem," said Hutch. "Maybe Gnick hit you with a magic impotence curse."

"Wait, can a cursed item put another curse on someone?" asked Starsky. "Wouldn't the two curses cancel each other out?"

"Like a double negative? That's a good question. What do you think, Marlin?"

"I'm not impotent!" Marlin shouted. He took a deep breath. "Rose is just...Rose. But even if I were, it has nothing to do with this."

"We'll be the judge of that, Marlin."

"Fine. The point is, I've been under a lot of stress, but I'm not crazy. Gnick killed those cats." He looked at the mirror. "And the dogs." He looked back at the detectives. "And now I'm afraid he's done something with Marlin Jr., but instead of looking for him, you're in here badgering me. I wish there were some way I could make you believe me!"

"There is, Marlin," Hutch said.

"There is?"

"Sure. Just push that button." He pointed to the table.

In front of Marlin sat a box with a big red button and a sign that said, "Push Me!" Had it been there the whole time? No, surely he'd have noticed a box like that, wouldn't he? Of course, he *had* been under a lot of stress lately. "Where'd this come from?" he finally asked.

"It doesn't matter where it came from, Marlin," said Hutch. "All that matters is once you push it, we'll believe you and we'll start looking for Marlin Jr."

"You will?"

"We will."

"Promise?"

"Promise."

Marlin put his hand on the button. "What about Gnick?"

"What about him?" asked Starsky.

"What will happen to him?"

"What do you care? He's a cat killer."

"And a dog killer."

"And you think he may have killed your son," Hutch added. "I'm surprised you're even worried about him."

Marlin looked at Gnick, flipped him off, and pushed the button.

"Are you ready to go?" he asked the officers.

"Ready to go?" asked Starsky. "We're ready to arrest you."

"But I pushed the button," said Marlin. "You said you'd believe me if I pushed the button! You promised!"

"Button? What button?" asked Hutch.

"It was right here!" Marlin said, pointing at the empty tabletop. Where was the button? "You said if I pushed it, you'd believe me and we'd start looking for Marlin Jr. So I pushed it. Can we go now?"

The speaker crackled back to life. *"Deus ex machina, Marlin? Really?"*

Marlin looked at the mirror. "What ex what?"

"It means 'god from the machine,'" said Hutch. "It happens when a writer's written himself into a corner, and rather than figure out a way to solve the problem, he intervenes in his own story and—"

The voice on the speaker interrupted. *"It could be a she. The writer could also be a she."*

Hutch rolled his eyes, then continued. "*She* intervenes in her own story and introduces a miracle to solve the problem."

"It's a real hack move, Marlin," said Starsky.

Marlin had no idea what they were talking about. "I don't understand," he said.

"You were stuck," said Hutch. "You knew we wouldn't believe your cursed killer gnome story. You'd tried fantasizing your way out of your present predicament, but that didn't work either. So, you imagined a button that would magically make us believe you and everything would turn out okay."

"But everything didn't turn out okay. I pushed it and—"

"And? Did we believe you?"

"No! The button didn't work!"

"That's your *deus*, Marlin. Not ours." Starsky stood up.

"It's also strike three. And do you know what happens at strike three?" He paused. "You're out."

Starsky pulled his gun and shot Marlin in the face.

***

Marlin sat up in bed. His sheets were soaked. He felt his forehead. No bullet hole. "Thank God it was all just a dream," he sighed.

"Oh, it wasn't *all* a dream, Marlin." Gnick threw Marlin Jr.'s bloody binky at Marlin. It bounced off his forehead and landed on his pillow. From across the hall, Rose screamed.

WELCOME TO COULROVILLE

Tom's pride kept him from looking at his phone as he tried to work his way home, but after several wrong turns and two literal dead ends, and with sunset more than a few hours in the rearview, he finally admitted defeat. For only the second time since he'd earned his driver's license, he'd have to stop and find a motel.

Over the years, he'd discovered there weren't many problems that couldn't be solved by a day spent cruising the back roads on autopilot, his only provisions a cooler of Diet Coke and his "Awesome Mix Tape Volume 3" CD.

Yesterday afternoon, his boss had given him the weekend to come up with a plan to ensure his team didn't miss their quota for a third straight month. So this morning he'd gassed up and hit the road. By the time he'd devised a strategy to sort out his sideshow of a sales force, he was deep in the heart of nowhere.

Just the way he liked it.

Of course, finding a solution was only half the fun for Tom. To complete the ritual, he'd challenge himself to find his way home by intuition. The rules were simple: no maps, no asking for directions, and no phone, except for emergencies.

Only once, and this was back in the days before GPS, had he found himself so lost he'd had to check into a motel for the night. Sitting on a lumpy bed with a slice of cold pizza and a ruler, things had taken a turn for the weird. According to the mileage charts, which he'd checked against three different maps and a wire-bound road atlas, it was impossible for him to have traveled as far as he had in just one day. He chalked it up to a backwoods wormhole and called it a night.

That's what made giving up tonight so hard. Truth be told, though, he just didn't have the energy to drive much longer. He pulled over, got out of the car to stretch his legs, and turned on his phone.

No bars.

No worries. He'd go another ten miles and try again. He hopped back in the car and turned the key. Nothing happened. He turned it again. And again. Still nothing. He thought for half a second about popping the hood, but you could fit what he knew about cars on the side of a pocket wrench, which he wouldn't know how to use anyway.

Maybe it was time to worry.

He got back out and leaned against the car. The engine ticked loudly as it cooled. It'd been at least an hour since he'd seen another car, so there was no telling how long it would be until someone drove by. A dim glow over the trees teased the possibility of a town somewhere up ahead. If he left on foot now, fingers crossed, a gas station would be open when he finally made it there. Fingers double-crossed, they'd have a working phone, and something better to eat than the burrito he'd snarfed down at his last pit stop.

At least the weather was nice.

He started walking, the full moon above the trees lighting his way. He listened to the night sounds as he went. Chirping crickets, an occasional croaking frog, the comforting clunk of his boot heels hitting the pavement. He filled in the final details of his new work plan along the way.

A high-pitched bird-song—*whip-poor-will!*—made him jump. Whippoorwills were bad luck, right? He pulled out his phone to look it up. Still no bars. How was that even possible? Wasn't "Thou shalt have Wi-Fi" written somewhere in the Constitution? If not, it should be. He made a note to call his congressperson as soon as he got a signal.

About twenty minutes later, he passed a billboard promising family fun in Coulroville, three miles ahead. At his present pace, he'd be there within the hour.

He'd walked another half mile or so when he saw the first homemade sign. Hand painted and nailed to a tree, it read: *Oh Won't You Stop*. No phone number, no URL, not even a logo. Tom didn't know what to make of it. It wasn't long until he came upon a second sign: *At Our Big Top*. Another quarter mile, another sign: *The Break Will Do You Well*. He smiled. It was like the old Burma Shave signs he'd seen on road trips when he was a kid. He looked forward to the next one. That anticipation turned sour when he read it: *Such Wretched Sights*. The next sign was even worse: *And Rancid Smells*. Was this some kind of joke? By the time he reached the payoff sign (*An Eternity In Hell!*) he wished he'd stayed in the car.

He was about to turn back and take his chances waiting on a good Samaritan when a snatch of music floated up from somewhere ahead. It reminded him of a merry-go-round, or maybe an ice cream truck. It didn't last long enough to place the tune. At least it wasn't a banjo.

A whiff of buttered popcorn tickled his nose. And not the cheap microwave stuff either, but the good movie theatre kind, soaked in that carcinogenic butter researchers said caused popcorn lung. Where could it be coming from way out here? Was the circus in Coulroville this week? That would explain the signs. Sort of. He felt a little better and kept walking.

Finally, light from a convenience store sign peeked through the trees up ahead.

Something scuffled along the pavement behind him. He turned, but there was nothing there. He started walking again, a little faster than before. Immediately, the scuffling noise returned. The steps shuffled, then flopped, like someone trying to walk in shoes that were too big for their feet. He turned around, more quickly this time, but the road was empty. He picked up his pace. Another five minutes and he'd be at the store.

A sharp brassy honk pierced the night. The scuffling started again. He stole a glance over his shoulder. The road was still clear. Who—or what—was making that noise? He jogged now. *Honk! Honk! Honk!* A series of rapid, overlapping honks filled the air, as if a flock of geese were flying overhead. Instinctively, he ducked.

Just as he reached a sign marking the town limits (*Welcome to Coulroville, Population: 217 Smiles and Counting!*) a cannon exploded behind him. Tom screamed, then ran full-sprint toward the store. His boots slapped hard against the asphalt. Glitter and confetti floated down around him as he ran, sticking to his hair and arms. Harsh, high-pitched, maniacal laughter echoed through the trees, punctuated by more honking. The sounds were coming from all around him now.

He made it to the parking lot and headed straight for the door. A sign hanging above the handle read *Back in 10 minutes!* with a childish smiley face drawn underneath. Running too fast to stop, Tom braced himself for impact, but the door was unlocked and swung open when he hit it.

"Help!" he yelled as he ran his hands along the door, looking for the latch. He twisted it shut, locking himself in. "Help!" he yelled again, louder this time. "Someone's after me!" He looked outside. The parking lot was empty. A few pieces of glitter sparkled as they floated down under the arc sodium lights.

Tom backed away from the door and turned toward the register. There was nobody behind the counter, just another *Be right back!* sign, decorated with an even more elaborate smiley face. This one looked like a clown from a child's nightmare: red nose, yellow eyes, curly blue hair, and big, pointy teeth. Next to the sign sat a bouquet of large, Day-Glo colored flowers. As Tom leaned over the counter to look for a phone, a stream of cold liquid sprayed out from the biggest flower, hitting him in the face. He jumped back and fell against a rack of Twinkies, frantically wiping his eyes.

It was just water.

He wiped his face with the sleeve of his shirt and headed toward the food station for some napkins. The shelves were filled with bags of circus peanuts and cotton candy, boxes of Cracker Jack and animal crackers. A mostly empty magazine rack displayed a few issues of something called *Clowning Around*. Multi-colored streamers hung from the ceiling. A hotdog roller warmed a handful of dogs, brats, and sausages. Tom's stomach gurgled. The florescent lights flickered and buzzed, then went out, plunging the store into darkness. Tom jumped. His elbow hit the hot dog rack and spilled condiments all over the floor.

Outside, a Volkswagen Beetle polka-dotted in rainbow colors screeched into the parking lot, momentarily lifting on two wheels and nearly slamming into one of the gas pumps. As soon as all four wheels were back on the pavement, the driver's door flew open and an impossibly tall clown climbed out. Another clown followed. Then another. And another. The parking lot soon filled with clowns of all shapes and sizes: beanpole, beach ball, rectangle, parallelogram. Each wore a brightly colored, ill-fitting suit and masked themselves in slashes of vivid greasepaint grotesquery. The driver raised a bicycle horn above his head and honked it. Once. Twice. Three times. The clowns snapped to attention. They penguin-waddled up to the store's windows and peered into the darkness.

Tom crouched below the hotdog roller. Slowly, he backed up toward the rear of the store. He'd almost reached the end of the aisle when he tripped on the condiment rack he'd just knocked over. He grabbed at a shelf to keep from falling but pulled an endcap display over instead. It hit the floor with a loud *clang!*

Tom sat on the floor in the darkness and prayed the clowns didn't hear it.

They did.

The impossibly tall clown who drove the Beetle grabbed the door handle and pulled. The latch held. He pulled again, harder this time. It wouldn't open. He stepped back to reassess the situation, then pointed at a short, bowling-ball shaped clown, who rolled up to the door and knocked. The first tap was playfully light, but each successive knock grew more violent until Tom feared the glass would break. He slid on his butt toward the rear of the store.

The florescent lights flickered again. When they came on, Tom's heart sank. He'd left a scattered trail of candy bars and a butt-sized smear of ketchup, mustard, and relish behind. The tall clown at the door saw Tom. He raised his horn and honked. The other clowns, crusted in blood and gore, raised their horns and honked back. Slowly at first, then faster and faster. Tom scrambled to his feet and stumbled toward the back, all thoughts of stealth gone. The lights turned off. Immediately, the honking stopped. Tom looked toward the front of the store.

The clowns were gone.

He pulled his phone out and tapped the flashlight app. There had to be something in the backroom he could use as a weapon. Two large metal shelves were stocked with paper towels, toilet paper, and cleaning supplies. There was a broom and dustpan leaning against the wall, next to a mop, bucket, and a *Caution: Wet Floor* sign. In the far corner was a small desk. Three of the drawers were empty, but in the fourth, beneath a well-thumbed copy of *Big Top Boobies*, he found a gun. Great. What Tom knew about guns you could write on the side of a bullet, which he wouldn't know how to load anyway.

Knock, knock.

Another light tapping, this time from somewhere *inside* the store. The knocking picked up in speed and intensity, a death metal drum solo that echoed in the empty store. Tom peeked around the corner. His phone lit up the room enough to see the ice freezer bouncing off the ground with each bang. The lights came back on and the banging stopped. Tom held his breath.

The freezer door slowly swung open. The tall clown unfolded himself from within and stepped out into the room. He stood at attention and honked his horn. One after another, the clowns from the parking lot climbed out and huddled together. Every time a new pair of floppy shoes touched the ground, they honked their horns in greeting. When the freezer was empty, a conga line of clowns snaked through each aisle until the store was full.

The tall clown waddled up to Tom. He pantomimed choking on something. A Victorian clown wearing a yellow rain slicker gave him the Heimlich maneuver. On the first squeeze, he coughed up an already inflated red balloon. On the second, he coughed up five more in quick succession. He thanked his pal, then pulled a seventh out of his ear. He was so focused on tying them into a long snake, he didn't notice Tom had pointed the gun at his head until it was too late. The other clowns mimed a collective gasp. Tom pulled the trigger.

A brightly colored flag displaying the word *"Bang!"* popped out.

The tall clown fell back into the arms of two shorter clowns, then bounced up and stared down at Tom. He shook his head and made a *tsk* motion with his fingers.

Before Tom could move, the tall clown grabbed his shirt and yanked him forward. He jammed the balloon snake into Tom 's mouth. Tom fought back, but two muscular clowns with Popeye arms grabbed him and held him still. A third yanked his head back to open his throat wider. He tried to bite the balloons, but his teeth bounced off them. As the tall clown forced the balloons down Tom's throat, Tom's body quivered, then convulsed. The Popeyes let go of him, and he collapsed. His body spasmed across the floor and the conga line clowns honked their horns in unison, timing each honk with his movements. As his seizures slowed, so did their honking, until he passed out.

***

The store was empty when Tom woke up. He had no idea how long he'd been out. He tried to sit, but the room spun too much, and he had to lie still for a few minutes. He clenched his jaw, willing himself not to throw up.

He took a deep breath and sat up again. The spinning was a bit more manageable this time. It had to have been a food poisoning dream, right? He thought that burrito had tasted funny. At least he'd have a great icebreaker before he unveiled his new sales strategy on Monday.

He reached up to grab a shelf for balance and froze. His hands were encased in white, puffy, three-fingered gloves. They wouldn't come off.

What the actual fuck?

He tried to stand, but tripped over his new Sasquatchian red and yellow clown shoes. He rolled over and crawled to the beer cooler. He finally managed to stand by leaning against the glass. When he saw his reflection, he froze. He didn't recognize the man who looked back. Spiky blue hair. A bright red ball for a nose. Skin a ghastly shade of fish belly white, with black greasepaint eyebrows that made him look perpetually surprised. Someone had swapped his jeans and Blue Öyster Cult concert tee for a pair of baggy checked pants, rainbow suspenders, and a striped puffy shirt.

In the glass he saw a long, spindly arm unwind from within the ice freezer behind him. He turned and watched as it stretched across the room, stopping a few inches from his face. Its index finger curled up in a clear invitation, beckoning him to follow. A calliope song floated up from somewhere deep in the freezer, accompanied by the smell of popcorn. Tom tried to argue, but no sound came out, so he just mouthed the word *No!* over and over again. He turned to run, but tripped over his floppy shoes. The hand grabbed him by the hair and pulled him toward the freezer. A dozen more arms snaked out and wrapped around his chest and neck, dragging him across the floor. His head smacked hard against a shelf, and he struggled to stay conscious. With one final tug, they pulled him into the freezer. The lights went out, and the door slammed shut, trapping him in the darkness.

***

KA-THUMP!

Christa slammed on her brakes. Had she hit a deer? She knew she zoned out when she drove, but she hadn't been asleep. Just lost in her thoughts about finally getting up the nerve to leave Jack. She turned off the radio, cutting off the guitar solo to "Comfortably Numb" in mid-note, and took a deep breath, which sounded too loud in the resulting silence.

What had she hit? She checked the rearview mirror. A small shape, too small to be a deer, lay in the road. A raccoon, maybe? She put on her hazards and got out of the car. She grabbed a piece of wood from the ground near her rear tire. *Just in case*, she told herself. She aimed her phone's flashlight app at the dark shape.

What the hell?

It was a pair of shoes. Giant red clown shoes.

Did she actually run over a pair of clown shoes? What were they doing out here in the middle of nowhere? She tossed them to the side of the road. At least she hadn't killed an animal. She turned toward her car and saw a road sign she hadn't noticed before. Wow, she really must've been in a daze. Not good. Well, a town meant coffee, and she could use a cup or three. And some food. Besides, the place sounds friendly, she thought as she read the sign.

Welcome to Coulroville, Population: 218 Smiles and Counting!

She got back in the car and put it in gear.

Maybe she'd even spend the night.

LOST AT LAST

"Sure you don't want to come with?" I already knew the answer, but I had to ask.

Chuck laughed, then answered with a question of his own. "How long we been friends, Wayne? Ten years?"

"Give or take."

"And in all that time, have I ever agreed to 'come with' on one of your hikes?" He made air quotes around "come with."

"No, but there's a first time for everything."

"Not for this, there isn't. I'm too old to go hiking with you and Sammie." Sammie lifted her head at the mention of her name. "No offense, Sam." He pointed his finger at me. "And whether or not you want to admit it, you're getting up there too."

"We'll see about that." I got up from my seat on his porch and walked down the driveway to my Jeep, Sammie on my heel. I opened the door and helped her into the passenger seat. The fact that she might be getting too old for our hikes wasn't something I was ready to admit either.

I slid behind the wheel and rolled down my window. "We still on for tonight? Or are you too old for steak and beers now too?"

Chuck laughed. "The day I'm too old for steak and beer is the day I meet St. Peter. You be careful out there. Try not to get lost."

It was my turn to laugh. He said that every time we left, even though I'd been hiking our part of the Arapaho for nearly twenty years. Probably knew those trails better than our town's volunteer search and rescue team. The day I couldn't find my way home was the day I'd meet St. Peter too.

Chuck waved as we pulled out of the driveway. I honked the horn and Sammie barked goodbye.

That was the last time we ever saw him.

***

It took about fifteen minutes to reach the Delain Gulch trailhead. Being a Tuesday morning, there were only a few cars in the parking area. They all had out-of-state plates.

I opened the door for Sammie. She was so excited, I didn't even have to help her down. I pretended not to notice her wince when she landed.

"Hold on, Sammie," I told her. "We have to put your leash on first." She gave me an exasperated look. "I know, but I don't make the rules. Got some out-of-towners here today, and I don't want to get reported again. Once we get to the fork, I promise I'll take it off, okay?"

The fork in question was about two miles from the parking lot. I figured the altitude would prevent any of these tourists from making it that far. And all the locals knew Sammie, so I wasn't worried about any of them turning us in.

The hike up to the fork was easy. We'd done it so many times over the years I was on autopilot, stepping over exposed roots more by memory than observation. Chuck's comment nagged at me more than it should. Okay, I wasn't as spry as I used to be, but I took relatively good care of myself, all things considered. No reason I shouldn't be able to keep doing this for another fifteen, twenty years at least.

Sammie's bark when we reached the fork snapped me out of my funk. True to my word, I unclipped her leash. She bolted straight up the right fork without looking back. She wouldn't go too far on her own, so I took my time following her. I could hear her up ahead trampling through the scrub. A few minutes later, I saw her digging around a spot to the side of the trail.

"Whatcha got, girl?" I asked as I caught up to her.

I reached down to see what she'd been playing with. It was some kind of animal skeleton, but not like anything I'd ever seen before. Body about the size of my hand. Wide jaw. Two rows of teeth. Six legs. There were a few tufts of fur scattered on the ground.

Thank goodness it was dead when she found it.

I always brought a few plastic grocery bags with me to pick up any trash I saw on the trails, so I took a couple pictures with my phone, then bagged it and tied it onto my pack. I hoped someone at the university would know what it was. I sure as hell didn't.

Sammie sat patiently on the trail, eager to get moving again. I bent down to pull some leaves from her fur and a flash of white jumped out at me from further back in the trees. I pushed through the brush to see what it was. Ten yards off the main trail, I found an old sign for the Eris Ridge Trail leaning sideways toward the ground.

I pulled out my trail map. There was no Eris Ridge Trail marked on it. No surprise there. I'd hiked by this very spot lord knows how many times, and I'd never even seen the sign before.

As I lifted the sign off the ground, two aspens about twenty yards deeper still caught my eye. Actually, what caught my eye was a dark space *between* the two aspens. Shafts of sunlight died at its edges, giving the blackness depth and shape, almost as if I were looking into a tunnel.

I took a step forward, and the darkness faded away, revealing a barely there path that led deeper into the woods. Woods that, until a few minutes ago, I thought I knew every inch of.

Sammie started toward the new path, but I grabbed her and clipped the leash back on her collar. She grunted in exasperation. "Better safe than sorry," I said.

I went back and tied an orange ribbon onto an aspen back on the main trail, and another on an aspen at the start of this new trail.

"Getting too old for this, are we, Chuck?" I said to myself. "Come on, Sammie, let's see what kind of trouble we can get into."

We headed in.

A few yards onto the path, the air grew thicker, more humid. It weighed down on my shoulders, almost holding me in place. "You feel that, Sammie?" I whispered. She pawed at the ground. I was about to turn back when my ears popped and everything returned to normal.

As we started walking again, I told myself it had to be a trick of the light. Trails didn't just magically appear. And that thing with the air? Some weird microclimate, right? Nothing to worry about.

By the time we'd gone another half a mile, I'd forgotten all about it.

***

We'd been walking for about an hour when my phone rang.

"What's up, Chuck?" It was an old joke, but it always made me smile. "You should've come with. You're not gonna believe this, but I found an old forgotten trail that's not on any map. Well, technically Sammie helped find it, and—"

"Jesus, you're alive! Where have you been?" His voice was so loud I had to hold the phone away from my ear.

"Of course I'm alive. What are you talking about?"

"Wayne, you've been gone for four days."

"Four days? Did you start drinking without me? You didn't eat my steak too, did you?" I laughed and looked at my watch. "We've been gone about two and a half hours total, the last hour or so on this new trail I've been trying to tell you about. I've snapped a few pictures I'll show you when we get back."

"Two and a half hours? Did you fall and hit your head? You left Tuesday morning. It's Friday afternoon now."

"Come on, Chuck, is this some kind of joke?"

"I'm not joking. I wasn't too worried when you didn't show up Tuesday night. I was hoping maybe you met a cute little trail bunny, and I thought, *good for him*. But when you still hadn't come home by Wednesday afternoon—"

"Wednesday afternoon?" I cut him off. "I'm telling you, we left the house this morning. *Tuesday* morning."

"And I'm telling you, it's Friday afternoon now. Every time I called, your phone clicked and then disconnected. I couldn't even leave a message. I drove out looking for you. Found your Jeep, so I walked up the trail."

I smiled at Sammie. "Wait, you actually went hiking? Now I *know* you're pulling my leg."

He huffed. "I was worried my best friend might be lost or hurt. Sue me. About a mile in, my knees reminded me why I never come with."

"So now I'm your best friend? Laying it on pretty thick, aren't you?"

I knew he was up to something, but it was still nice to hear him say it. Especially after his earlier dig about my age. Guys don't share that stuff nearly often enough. Truth be told, he was my best friend too. I was a wreck after Lori's accident. She was my north star, and I was lost without her. But Chuck helped me find my way back from a very dark place. Hiking with Sammie helped too, of course.

Funny thing was, I'd never wanted a dog, but when Lori found Sammie wandering down a trail, she insisted we keep her. Poor girl was a mess. Skinny, matted fur, tapeworms. Despite all that, it was love at first sight for Lori. It took me a little longer, but I can't imagine life without her now. We hung flyers, posted on social media, checked the pound, even ran an ad in the paper, but nobody claimed her. Looking back, it's like Sammie knew I would need her, and that's why she found us when she did. Because a few months after that, Lori was gone.

Chuck sighed. "Anyway, I called the sheriff. He laughed me off at first, but when you still hadn't shown up by Thursday morning, he organized a search party. Felt like half the town showed up." He lowered his voice. "Even Ted Marsh came out."

My body stiffened. "Okay, Chuck, this was kind of cute at first, but you crossed the line. Best friend, my ass. Why would you say something like that?"

Ted Marsh was the bastard who'd hit Lori. She'd been walking home from work one evening when he ran a stop sign. Of course, he was drunk. Just like his old man. Spent six years in prison, then got out on parole. I nearly lost it when he moved back. Asshole lives with his brother a few miles outside town now. Bags groceries at the Safeway. I shop at the King Soopers fifteen miles away to avoid him. People say he's changed. Goes to church and everything. I don't believe it. People like Ted Marsh don't change.

Chuck knew he'd struck a nerve. "Look, I'm sorry," he said. "Just don't hang up, okay? I'm sending you some pictures."

My phone dinged. The pictures were coming through. I put the call on speaker and thumbed through them as we talked.

"What am I looking at, Chuck?"

The first image showed three guys from my bowling league, standing next to my Jeep at the trailhead. Someone had written "Where R U Wayne?" in the dust on the back window. The next image was of the sheriff. He had a topographic map of the Arapaho National Forest spread across the hood of his SUV. He'd circled the area around the Delain Gulch Trail. After that were a few more shots of other locals, including Ted fucking Marsh, walking a search line. What the hell?

The last one was the kicker though. It was the front page of our local paper, the one Lori used to write for. Chuck had zoomed in on the masthead's date. It was Friday, three days from today.

Despite the sun's warmth, a cold bead of sweat ran down my back.

"I don't know what the hell's going on," I said, rubbing my temples as I spoke. Maybe I *had* fallen down and hit my head. "I swear we've only been on this trail an hour or so."

"Which trail? We'll come find you."

"That's just it. I'd never heard of it. Like I said, Sammie helped find it. It's not on my map. That's why I was so excited about hiking it. A chance to explore something new for a change. We've seen a few weird things so far, like this freaky little skeleton Sammie found, but it's been pretty straightforward since then."

"What can tell me about it?"

"The skeleton or the trail?"

"Let's stick with the trail for now."

"It's called Eris Ridge. Barely there to start, then it gets a little more established. Still grown over in spots. Moderate altitude gain. Nothing out of the ordinary. The Peak's always been on our left."

"Okay, that helps. How do we find it?"

I told him where to look, but not about the dark tunnel that stretched between the aspens, or how the trail appeared out of nowhere, or how it felt like we'd pushed through some kind of barrier when we started out. Those things I kept to myself.

"I tied an orange ribbon around an aspen a ways up the right fork of the Delain Gulch Trail," I said. "Keep an eye out for the trail sign. I tried to stand it back up, but it may have fallen down again. The Eris Ridge Trail is maybe thirty yards back from that. I tied another orange ribbon on an aspen where it starts."

"Right at the fork. Orange ribbon. Old sign off the main trail. Got it." I could see him making a mental checklist as he spoke. He'd spent his career in logistics before retiring a few years back, so I knew he'd keep the details straight. "You turn around now and head back, okay?" he said. "We're gonna get you out of there."

He hung up.

I tugged Sammie's leash. "Come on, Sammie. It's time to go home."

Normally she'd argue with me—she enjoyed hiking as much as I did—but I think she knew something was wrong with the trail we were on.

It only took us another minute or two to realize just how wrong.

My phone rang again. It was Chuck. He sounded more worried than last time. "Where are you? Did something happen? We've been waiting here for over an hour."

"An hour? Chuck, you literally just hung up with me. Sammie and I have walked maybe fifty yards since then."

"Shit." He was silent for a moment. I checked my phone to make sure we hadn't been disconnected. "We found your orange ribbons, but…" His voice trailed off.

"But what?"

"But there's no trail sign. No Eris Ridge Trail."

"Are you sure you're in the right spot?"

"I'm sure." He sent me a photo of the first orange ribbon.

Sammie growled, deep and low.

"I have to call you back. Something's up with Sammie."

I heard him yell, "Don't you hang up on me!" as I hung up on him.

Sammie was sniffing the air and turning in circles. Her hackles stood up, and she howled. I normally loved the sound of her howl, but this one made me nervous. When the echo died away, she tucked her tail and pressed herself against my leg, shivering. She shook her head back and forth, then tilted it in confusion.

I was confused too. The trail didn't look the same as it had when I answered the phone. The trees were taller, thicker, closer to the path. The rocks were different too. A minute ago there were basketball-sized chunks of granite scattered on either side of the trail. Now they were flatter, round and smooth, like river rocks. And while the air had smelled of pine all morning, now I smelled salt, like we were near the ocean.

I don't have to tell you there are no oceans in Colorado.

Whatever happened to Sammie had passed. She looked up at me like everything was normal, tongue out, eyes happy and bright. I took a deep breath to calm my nerves. The last thing I needed out here was a panic attack. It was easy enough to lose your bearings on a trail you knew, let alone one you'd never hiked before. Chuck's story was a little harder to explain, but nothing we couldn't sort out over beers later tonight. I decided I'd walk for half an hour and then call him back. The Peak was on my left coming out, so as long as I kept it on my right going back, we should be good.

We didn't make it five minutes before Chuck called again.

I answered on the first ring. "What's going on, Chuck? Did you find the trail?" I knew I sounded a little too anxious, but I didn't care. I needed answers.

"No." He hesitated. "Listen, Wayne, the sun's gone down, and there are storms moving in. Sheriff says it's too dangerous to stay out here tonight. My knees agree with him."

"What are you talking about? It's sunny and warm here. There's not a cloud in the sky."

I pretended not to hear the thunder on Chuck's end of the call.

"I'm sorry, man. Look, I'm sleeping in my van down in the parking lot if you make it out. I'll come back up here in the morning and keep looking if you don't."

I heard another loud clap of thunder through the phone, and the line went dead.

I sat down on an overturned log. My head was spinning, my hands shaking. None of this made any sense. I needed to calm myself down before I spiraled. I closed my eyes and focused on my breathing. Slow and steady, in through the nose and out through the mouth, the way Lori had taught me. Once my heart rate slowed down, I took a drink from my water bottle, then poured a little in Sammie's silicone bowl, making a mental note of how much we had left. Just in case.

Sammie lapped hers up and looked at me for more.

"Sorry, buddy, but that's enough for now, okay?"

I opened a granola bar and broke her off a piece. She gobbled it down, then laid her head on my foot.

The panic was still there, flitting about the edge of my thoughts, looking for weak spots in my defenses, but the worst had passed. I was back in control. I sat for a few minutes longer and watched a line of clouds slowly drift into view. A flock of birds flew through them. As one, they banked from left to right. I followed them with my eyes.

And saw the Peak was gone.

***

It's impossible to say how far we've walked on this trail. Or how long we've been walking. Space and time are different out here. Sometimes it leads us in a straight line. Sometimes it feels like we're going in circles. Sometimes uphill, sometimes down. Sometimes both simultaneously. I know that doesn't make any sense, but I don't know how else to describe it.

We've walked below jagged cliffs carved from a type of rock I can't identify. Alongside canyons with no visible bottom. Over dunes on the beach of an ancient seabed. One minute we can be on the plains; five minutes later we're atop a mountain. Once, I turned around to look at a rock formation I thought I recognized. But the trail behind us had already changed.

That gave me an idea for a video. First, I shot myself talking to the camera. "What's up, Chuck, or whoever finds this?" I said. "I know it sounds crazy, but sometimes this trail changes when you're not looking. Scared the crap out of me the first few times it happened, but we're kind of used to it now. Right, Sammie?" She barked when I said her name.

"Don't believe me? Watch this." I pointed the camera away from me. "See those trees up ahead? Four pines, grouped together. See the rocks scattered around? Now, watch what happens when I turn away." I slowly turned around, keeping the camera aimed straight ahead. When I completed the circle, the pine trees and rocks were gone. A raspberry bush and some scrub oak had replaced them. I grabbed a handful of berries, then turned the camera back to my face. "Have fun figuring that one out." I shot quite a few videos like that in the beginning. They helped keep the panic in check as I processed what was happening.

We've seen plenty of wildlife along the way. Most of it's been recognizable. None of it seems to pose any threat. I let Sammie catch some squirrels and rabbits when our granola ran out. She's caught a few of those little six-legged critters too. Of course, they taste like chicken.

She enjoys the hunt, although I never let her go too far off the trail. And I always put aside a little meat for jerky. My flint striker promised four thousand strikes when I bought it, but I've had it for years, so who knows how much longer it'll last. I can use my glasses as a magnifying glass, but that only works when the sun's out. I need to figure out how to start one by rubbing two sticks together.

We haven't seen any people. But I'm not giving up hope. Evidence of others is everywhere. A brick fireplace marking the site of an old homestead. The remnants of a deserted frontier town, its occupants long lost to time. Primitive altars to unknown gods. Once, we passed the crumbled remains of a giant statue, only the base and part of the right foot and ankle were still intact. It had four toes. At one point, the dirt path became a paved road. There were several cars abandoned on the berm. I didn't recognize the make or model of any of them. If they'd had anything worth scavenging, somebody had beat me to it. Eventually, we stopped at an old Koko brand gas station. A faded sign featuring its mascot, a black border collie with a bright red collar, hung cockeyed in the dusty front window. I looked inside for food and water, but the shelves were empty, the tap long dry.

Not far from the station, the road cut through a massive cornfield. I threw several ears in my pack. The rustling of the stalks sounded like whispers in a language I didn't understand. In the distance, iron giants, frozen in place, towered over the rows. Skeletons hung from their multiple arms, slowly swinging in the breeze. Guess I knew where some of the people here ended up. I made Sammie pick up the pace until the road gave way to gravel and then back to dirt. Behind us, I heard the *screech* of rusted metal moving. We ran then, and didn't stop running until I was sure we'd gone deep enough into the forest that those giants couldn't get through. At least not without us hearing them first.

I knew sleep would be impossible that night, so I pushed us until well after sunup the next morning. It was slow going in the dark, but I wanted to put as much space as possible between us and those killing machines. I hadn't come this far to end up swinging on the end of a rope.

I still checked my phone periodically. Usually, it had zero bars. A few times, it had seven. I could never get a call to go through though. I took a lot of pictures and videos until my phone ran out of storage. Hopefully, it got backed up to a cloud at some point, but I'm not holding my breath on that one.

GPS was no help either. Most of the time, it couldn't find my location. And when it did work, it showed us near places I'd never heard of, like Rocky Point, Discordia, and Lake Hali. They'd disappear as soon as I turned in that direction.

Despite all that, I still had faith we'd make it out. Up until the day I broke my solar charger. After that, all I could do was watch, helplessly, hopelessly, as my phone's battery level dropped, severing our only tie to home. My charge was down to three percent when it rang for the last time.

"What's up, Chuck?" I tried to make myself sound normal. I don't think it worked.

"You're still alive!" He didn't try to hide the shock in his voice. "I'd about given up hope."

"You can't get rid of me that easy."

"It's been six months now, Wayne." He sounded exhausted. "I still try calling every few days, but this is the first time I've got through. How are you? *Where* are you?"

I thought for a moment. "All things considered, not that bad. In a weird way, I'm kind of enjoying myself. No idea where I am though. You ever hear of a Lake Hali?"

"Nope."

"Me neither. But that was the last landmark that showed up on my GPS. How are things back home?"

"Well, I'm pretty sure the bank's gonna foreclose on your house soon. Saw some suits poking around the other day, peeking in the windows. Asked if I knew where you were. I told 'em to get the hell off your property. One of them gave me his card, if you want his number. I had your Jeep towed back to my place. It's under a tarp in the garage."

"They can have it," I said. "And you can keep the Jeep. It's the least I can do."

"You sound like you're not coming back," he said. "You're not giving up, are you?" He paused. "Sammie okay?"

"She's good. Say 'hi,' Sammie." I held the phone down to her. She barked. "Got a little spring back in her step, actually." I looked at my phone. The battery level was down to one percent. "I'm not giving up, I'm just not sure I can find my way back. My phone's about to die too. Not that it was much help. But this is probably the last time we'll get to talk."

"I feel so helpless," he said. "I can't get anyone to search with me anymore. Sheriff won't even bother returning my calls. I don't know what else to do."

I hated hearing him like this. "Nothing you can do, man." I struggled to hold back tears. "You've been a good friend, Chuck. The best, really. I'd have been lost without you after Lori passed."

"You'd have done the same for me." There was a hitch in Chuck's voice. "I'm gonna miss you, man."

"Me too."

"Hey, Wayne?" His voice grew fainter. Static popped and hissed over the speaker.

"Yeah?"

"Try not to get lost."

My phone died.

I laughed, despite my tears, and rubbed Sammie behind her ears. "Whaddaya say, girl? Wanna come with?" She looked up at me, eager to get back on the trail.

We're on top of a ridge now, overlooking a vast plain. Wonder if it's *the* Eris Ridge. I have no idea where we'll be an hour from now. A week. A year. What worlds we'll encounter. What sights we'll see. Maybe we'll find our way back, and Chuck and I can finally have that steak and beer. Or maybe St. Peter's waiting for me at the end of this trail. And maybe, just maybe, Lori will be there too.

It's a big maybe, but it's all I have. And that's good enough for now.

Story Notes

"That's What Friends Are For" Back in 2019, I took a LitReactor class on writing horror. (Surprise!) Brian Keene was one of four instructors that session. For his assignment, he wanted us to write the origin story for a famous horror villain. "The Boogeyman" by Uncle Steve is one of my favorite short stories, so I decided to write his origin story. I failed. Miserably. But Brian told me there was something interesting about the opening scene and I should keep working on that part. I did, and the resulting story ended up making the 2022 Preliminary Stoker ballot for Superior Achievement in Short Fiction. So nice…

"Strange Constellations" This story was produced by the NoSleep Podcast, which means it's the technically the only thing I've written that my wife has actually read, even though she listened to it. (Yes, listening to audiobooks IS reading.) She really liked it, which meant the world to me. A few years later, I went into a corn maze for the first time and discovered I mostly got it right.

"Fresh" The very first story I ever sold! ("Sold" is a relative term, since I think I only got five bucks for it.) But I think it holds up pretty well. Bar room trivia time: I wrote Lou as a demon, but pretty much everyone thinks he's a vampire. YMMV.

"Trash Talk" This story started as an exercise in Moanaria's Fright Club. (Side note: this is one of the best writing programs you can do, so you should do it.) Later, I ran across a call for an anthology featuring original monsters. "What's more original than a 90-foot tall sentient garbage dump?" I stupidly thought and sent it off into the ether. The next day I got a nice form rejection. When I went to enter it at Duotrope, I noticed their average rejection time was 18 days. Now, I can't math, which is why I write, but it seems to me they hated my story 18 times more than the average submission. I still love the story, though, and hope you do, too.

"Loop de Loop de Loop" Writing ads for nearly 30 years has taught me to write really, really short. (That's one of many reasons I don't think I have a novel in me.) Drabbles are only 100 words. Unless you're stuck in a time loop, in which case it's the same 100 words over and over and over...

"Reaching Bottom" Speaking of writing short, a lot of my stories start as flash fiction. The first draft of this story was only 600 words or so. I workshopped it in Fright Club and The Author's Journey program at Crystal Lake Publications (a bucket list publisher) and got it up to its present length. It's been shortlisted a couple of times that never panned out, which sucks because it's one of my favorite stories.

"Can You Dig It?" Another Fright Club story. The assignment was to write about a haunted object. I got put on the spot about what I was going to use, and in my panic blurted out "shovel!" It actually worked out pretty well. (But seriously, what's up with that wet dream sequence?)

"Sharing is Caring" Kinda goes without saying that I love Halloween, even though I just said it. The kids are all adorable little versions of famous monsters and killers, which was fun to write.

"The Outpost, Outside" This story was originally called "The Outpost" and was rejected a ton. I changed the name to something a little more highbrow and it immediately sold, which is funny because it's basically a story about me and my little brother fighting a cooties outbreak.

"The Santadvent Killer" Like the main character, I worked retail for six years when I was younger. And let me tell you, the Christmas Spirit is a myth. Unlike the title character, however, I didn't shove a Christmas tree up a mall Santa's butt. Or did I?

"The Space Between" After we left Colorado, we ended up in Omaha for a few years. At the time, we still owned a small cottage in the city of Idaho Springs that we rented out on VRBO. I would make the nine-hour drive once every couple of months (more often during ski season), and outside of corn fields and feed lots, there's a whole lot of nothing in the space between cities along I-80. This story made the Preliminary Stoker Ballot for Superior Achievement in Short Fiction in 2020.

"The Tunnel at the End of the Light" In 2015 I went to a writers retreat at the Stanley Hotel in Estes Park. All the attendees were invited to submit stories for an anthology about that weekend called The Frankenstein Experiment. (There were also plans for a reality show about the event.) My story, originally called "Koko," was picked for the anthology, but alas both projects died on the vine. That's okay, though, because I still made a lot of really good friends there. A lot of this story is autobiographical, although the names have been changed to protect the innocent.

"Necrophiliacs Anonymous" A lot of times my first draft is pretty much nothing but dialogue. This is one of those times. ("Trash Talk" started out this way, too.) After I was happy with all the necro jokes, I went back and started filling in all the details. Plus added a few more jokes. If you ever come to one of my readings in the future, there's a good chance I'll be reading this story. You've been warned.

"Meat Cute" A fun little piece of cannibal flash that got me on the cover of Red Room Magazine with Jack Ketchum and Tim Waggoner, so achievement level unlocked. I read this at StokerCon in Providence. Was I nervous about yelling "Stop staring at her tits!" to a room full of strangers? A little. But it got a great response, and afterward several people told me I should attend Necon, which I did and still do because Necon is friggin' awesome.

"Blind Spot" The idea for this story came to me one night when I was walking my dog Sammie around the block in Omaha. It took me a few years to figure out what to do with it, though. I shared an early draft with Rebecca Allred that was written in first person. Her critique was basically, "You can't write a story in first person where the main character dies. You suck!" When I told her that Neil Gaiman did it in "Click Clack the Rattle Bag," her response was basically, "You're no Neil Gaiman. You suck!" Point taken, Rebecca. (To be fair, I'm not sure if she said I suck twice, but it makes for a funnier story.)

"The World Ends at the World's End" I originally wrote this for an anthology that wanted two fairy tales mashed up. I ended up mashing three fairy tales with bits of Lovecraft and the King in Yellow. Even though the publisher liked the story, they rejected it because I can't follow directions. I ended up selling it to LOLcraft, which is a much better fit anyway.

"Nicholas" A cannibal Christmas story? Be still my beating heart. At this point you're probably wondering if I hate Christmas, and the answer is yes, yes I do.

"Caterwaul" Pseudopod is another bucket list market. I've come close a few times and received some nice personal rejections, but haven't cracked it yet. When they turned down this story, they said, "the interrogation room scene was ridiculously over the top, and we mean that in the nicest way possible." One of these days I should put that on a shirt.

"Welcome to Coulroville" Clowns are greasepainted freaks. Yeah, I said it.

"Lost at Last" My dog Sammie used to curl up under my desk when I was writing, and I miss her every day. The idea for this story came from a t-shirt I bought my wife in Breckenridge. It was an illustration of a hiker and his dog looking out over a mountain range with the caption "Lost at Last." I'm not a religious person, but the idea of spending the afterlife hiking around with Sammie sure sounds like Heaven to me.

ABOUT THE AUTHOR

Larry Hinkle is an advertising copywriter living in Rockville, Maryland with his wife and two doggos. He's an active member of the Horror Writers Association, and his stories made the preliminary Stoker ballot for Superior Achievement in Short Fiction in 2020 and 2022.